ELODIE

A TALE OF PASSION,
DARK SHADOWS
AND VANISHING SMILES

E.B. SANCHEZ

GLASSMILL PRESS
EBSANCHEZ.COM

This book is a work of fiction. Names, characters and incidents are the product of the author's imagination or are used fictitiously. Any resemblance to actual events or persons living or dead is coincidental.

ISBN 978-0-9970266-1-0 (print)
ISBN 978-0-9970266-2-7 (ebook)

Published by Glassmill Press
ebsanchez.com

Cover design by Monica Doyle

PUBLISHER'S CATALOGING-IN-PUBLICATION DATA
(Prepared by The Donohue Group, Inc.)

Names: Sanchez, E. B.
Title: Elodie : a tale of passion, dark shadows, and vanishing smiles / by E.B. Sanchez.
Description: [San Marcos, California] : Glassmill Press, [2017]
Identifiers: ISBN 978-0-9970266-1-0 (print) | ISBN 978-0-9970266-2-7 (ebook)
Subjects: LCSH: Women--Psychology--Fiction. | Flower arrangers--Psychology--Fiction. | Interpersonal relations--Fiction. | Depression in women--Fiction. | Nostalgia--Fiction. | LCGFT: Romance fiction. | Thrillers (Fiction)
Classification: LCC PS3619.A517 E56 2017 (print) | LCC PS3619.A517 (ebook) | DDC 813/.6--dc23

To RAUL,

whose love, caring and patience

have brightened my life

WITH LOVE

You cannot do a kindness

too soon,

for you never know how soon

it will be too late.

—RALPH WALDO EMERSON

CONTENTS

CONTENTS

ELODIE

1

The White Night

WINTER WAS COMING. Elodie felt it in her bones, and her heart was heavy. She feared winter with its snowstorms and endless gray skies. She feared the lonely days ahead with only her misery to keep her company. She sat in her big, faded chair in front of the cold fireplace that had not been lit in many years. A gaping black hole, frightening in its blackness, with a faint smell of soot from fires long ago that reminded her of happier times.

She turned her head and looked out of the window at the overcast sky. Somewhere the sun was shining, just not here. The tall trees were starting to shed their leaves. They were usually colorful, but not now. The leaves were mostly a dirty brown and slowly, ever so slowly sailed to the wet ground, much the world around Elodie passed by in slow motion. Suddenly, the wind picked up, and the falling leaves danced wildly to a tune that only they could hear. The thin tree branches bent and twisted, accompanying the feverish dance of the leaves. The house shuddered and groaned at the unexpected fierceness of the wind, and a howl rose from deep inside the thick forest, its tune carrying to Elodie's ears. She sat up, shaking with fear, and slowly got up and checked that all the windows and doors were shut and locked.

In the hallway, she passed the mirror and saw a strange, sad face staring at her with huge gray eyes sunken in their sockets, and gray hair that had long lost its luster framing the gaunt features. A high-pitched scream escaped from her throat, and it took a moment for her to realize that she was looking at her own reflection. She had covered the mirror with an old towel—she could not bear to look at herself and what had become of her—but a draft had shifted the thin towel, and it had fallen to the wooden floor. Elodie slowly picked it up and draped it once more over the mirror.

Shuffling back to her old chair, she slumped into it, grabbed the woolen blanket and covered herself. She sat there, gazing out the window at the darkness enveloping the world. There was no moon, and the stars were hiding behind the heavy clouds. She thought of the consolation of silence, of obscurity without images, of an eternity without future, of sleep without dreams and without awakening. Elodie dozed off and began to dream.

She was a young woman walking along the peaceful

lake where she had grown up. It was a warm, sunny spring day, and the red and yellow tulips were in full bloom. The freesias spread their unmistakable scent, and the trees stood tall in all their soft green splendor. Elodie was content.

She woke with a start when she bumped into something and found her white Angora cat on her lap. The dream lingered for a few seconds on the edges of her mind, but before she could recapture the happy feeling it had evoked, it dissipated.

Elodie got up and went upstairs to her bedroom, where she slipped between the cold sheets. These past few days, she had felt exhausted. She closed her eyes, hoping to go back to the sunny shore, but instead she found herself in a black forest with no way out. She twisted and turned around bushes and tall weeds, to no avail. A hanging strand of ivy wound itself around her throat and threatened to strangle her. The more she fought, the tighter the noose grew. With her last bit of strength, she pulled away from the ivy and fell heavily to the ground. She woke up with a scream and came to lying on the cold, hard wood floor, her heart pounding violently. Laboriously, she rose and decided to go for a walk, needing some air. She took her raincoat from the hall closet and opened the front door.

A biting wind hit her tired face, and the darkness swallowed her surroundings. A light snow started to fall, wetting her cheeks. Carefully, she stepped onto the walkway leading around the house to the forest. She stopped by the little bench her husband had made so many years ago and sat down. Staring into the darkness, she tried to recollect his features. She could not. Tears welled up behind her eyes but would not flow; years of suppressing them had clogged her tear ducts. Her face was moistened only by the snowflakes melting on her hot cheeks, forming small rivulets that ran along her chin and finally dropped onto the already-wet ground.

Will this torment never end? she silently asked the wind. But no answer was forthcoming.

2

The Early Days

ELODIE HAD MET him in Paris while she was studying French at the Sorbonne. Young and innocent, they were both full of curiosity about the world and what life had to offer. They were in love with France and its culture, and excited to be at a center of learning as prestigious as the Sorbonne, which offered several different certificates of proficiency in the French language.

They had met on a hot July day at the orientation for English-speaking students. Finding themselves assigned to the same class, they quickly realized they were both Americans hailing from the West Coast. His name was Hutch—short for Hutchinson—and Elodie was immediately drawn to the powerful young man. His light brown hair was stylishly coiffed, and he wore old blue jeans with a purple Nirvana T-shirt. He was very handsome, but his most stunning feature was his nose. Elodie had never seen a nose that perfect; it was straight with a narrow tip, and she longed to glide her fingers gently over it and feel its soft hardness. It fit Hutch's friendly face perfectly. His warm brown eyes shone with gentleness, but a hint of determination was hiding just below the surface.

When he asked her to join him for a cup of coffee after the presentation, Elodie accepted without hesitation. They found a quaint little street café where they ordered *beignets au chocolat* and hot coffee. Absorbed in conversation, they talked until the street lights turned on and it was time to go to their quarters. Luckily, they did not live far apart, as the university had arranged housing for them both.

During the eight weeks they spent in Paris, they were inseparable. They went to class together, did homework together and explored the city with its treasures. All too soon, the summer was over and they had to say good-bye. Hutch was going to travel around Europe for a few weeks, and Elodie was expected to return home by Labor Day weekend. They exchanged phone numbers and promised to stay in touch.

Upon her return to the United States, Elodie continued her studies in San Diego, graduating a year later from the University of California with a bachelor's degree in management science. Afterwards, unsure what to do with her life, she moved to California's central valley and took a job at a small local garden center, where she soon became part of the team. Elodie liked working there, especially when she was called to help prepare flower arrangements for special occasions. Silvanus, who also worked at the garden center, usually delivered the finished arrangements, and Elodie accompanied him sometimes. Over time, they became friends.

One day, while delivering wedding flowers in the old white pickup truck, he said shyly, "Elodie, we've been delivering flowers together for some time, and I would very much like to take you to lunch after we are done here."

"Yes, that would be nice. I've nothing planned for this afternoon," she answered absentmindedly, looking out the window.

They walked silently to a small deli not far from the garden center. Elodie had seen the deli sign before but had never bothered stopping to have lunch, or even a cup of coffee. As they approached, Silvanus turned to her.

"Thank you for coming to lunch with me," he said. "It's rather awkward to eat alone."

Elodie nodded. She knew exactly how he felt. She would often forego eating rather than sit in a restaurant alone.

They arrived at the cottage-like deli, and Silvanus opened the door for her. She was surprised when she saw the interior. She had expected a drab old place, but it was decorated with friendly, flowery wallpaper and white wainscoting all around the room. Against the back wall hung white shelves filled with bottles of different shapes and colors, as well as small jars, their contents hidden. They sat down by the window at a small table covered with a white tablecloth overlaid with a honey-colored table runner to finish the setting. Rosemary plants in white pots sat proudly in the middle of each table. Looking around, Elodie was amazed to find old sepia pictures on the walls depicting people dressed in stylish clothes from the early 1920s. The whole interior exuded an atmosphere of times long past.

Elodie closed her eyes for a moment, and her mind wandered back to Paris, to the little street cafes she and Hutch had visited so often during that memorable summer. *Where are you, Hutch?* she wondered, a small sigh escaping her throat. After she had graduated, she had dialed the phone number he had given to her in Paris, but an impersonal voice recording said that the number had been disconnected.

"What is it, Elodie?" Silvanus asked, concerned.

"Oh, nothing," Elodie replied. "This place just brings back memories of a summer a few years ago that I spent in Paris as a foreign-language student."

"I hope they're pleasant memories, despite your sigh," he said.

Elodie turned her gaze on him and really saw him for the first time. His square face was tanned by the unrelenting sun, and two trusty brown eyes looked out under dark, bushy eyebrows. His lips were full, though the set of his chin intimated a stubborn streak. His dark-brown hair was cropped short and stood out at all angles from his head. Elodie smiled; he reminded her of a little hedgehog.

"Why   are   you   smiling?"   Silvanus   asked

apprehensively.

"I guess a pleasant thought must have entered my mind," she answered casually.

Thankfully, the black-haired waitress came to take their order. Elodie ordered a Crannie Melt, consisting of chicken salad, cheddar cheese, cranberry sauce, and honey mustard on grilled sourdough, with a Diet Coke. Silvanus went for the Pesto Chicken, a grilled chicken breast, provolone cheese, hickory-smoked bacon, pesto sauce, lettuce, tomato, red onion, mayo and mustard on a toasted roll, and a glass of beer. It did not take long for the sandwiches to be served, and Silvanus and Elodie ate them, an uncomfortable silence stretching between them. Once finished, they both tried to talk at the same time, then stopped awkwardly.

"Please go ahead," Elodie said quickly.

"I just wanted to ask if you didn't like your sandwich, since you only ate half of it."

"It's a big sandwich, and I'd rather take the rest home and have it for dinner," she replied. She asked the waitress for a box and put her leftover sandwich in it.

Silvanus asked for the check, and they agreed to split the bill. They left the little café and silently walked back to the garden center. Elodie thanked him for his company and disappeared into the office before he could reply.

"What an awful lunch that was!" Elodie whispered to herself. "I must be a very boring person to go out with. We didn't even talk during lunch, and not much before or afterwards, either. I wonder, have I always been this way? Did Hutch think I was boring, too?"

There it was again, the thought of Hutch. She shook her head to clear her mind and busied herself in the office. Soon it was time to leave. Taking the sandwich box out of the refrigerator and carrying it carefully so as not to spill the contents, she put it on the passenger seat of her old gray Honda for the drive home. She parked on the wide street and walked up the steep stairs to her small apartment, which was on the second floor of a large building on the outskirts of the village. She had discovered it by chance and had liked it immediately. It was a one-bedroom apartment with an open-concept kitchen and a small bathroom. There was even a balcony; not large, but it had room for a couple of chairs and a small bistro table. When the weather was warm, she would often have her morning coffee outside while reading the local paper on her tablet.

Over the next few weeks, Elodie did not see Silvanus. That was fine with her; she did not know how to behave when he was around and was relieved not to run into him. One day, though, he came to the office to ask her to order some supplies for the garden shop. Business concluded, he started to walk out but turned at the door and looked at her.

"Elodie, we need to talk. Please have dinner with me on Friday evening. I'll pick you up at your place around seven."

Unable to think of an excuse, she said, "That would be lovely. See you Friday."

"What have I done?" she mumbled to herself. "A whole evening with Silvanus is going to be endless, and

I was looking forward to taking a long, hot bath, having a glass of red wine with my dinner, and going to bed early."

When Friday rolled around, Elodie found herself in a somber mood. She did not feel like going out with Silvanus but was too shy to tell him. So reluctantly, she got ready for dinner. She had no idea where they were going and what she should wear, but she decided on a dark-blue skirt with a white, long-sleeved blouse. When the doorbell rang, she put on her black Mary Janes, grabbed her cheap black purse and her black cardigan, and headed to the door. Silvanus was waiting for her by the entrance and handed her a box of chocolates.

"Hi, Elodie. I thought you might like some chocolates."

"Thank you, Silvanus, how thoughtful of you. I'll just take them up to the apartment," she said. She quickly ran upstairs and left the box on the kitchen counter, not bothering to unwrap it, then hurried back downstairs.

The sooner we leave, the sooner I'll be back home, she thought.

They walked to Silvanus's dark blue Acura, and he held the door open for her. The car had a leather interior and was impeccably clean inside and out. Elodie was impressed; her car was usually not so clean.

"Do you like Mexican food?" Silvanus asked her.

"Yes, I do," she answered. "Do you know a Mexican restaurant around here?"

"It's about a half hour drive. I hope you don't mind?"

"Of course not. I haven't had Mexican food in quite a

while."

The conversation stopped again, and Elodie once more regretted having accepted the invitation.

Maybe if I just start talking, that will loosen his tongue, Elodie thought. So she started telling him about her life as a student at the university, her travels and her hobbies. Silvanus listened to her but still said nothing, and Elodie felt her anger rising at having to carry the conversation on her own.

Soon they arrived at the Mexican restaurant. It had colorful flags outside and flower boxes in the windows. The door was open, and a mouthwatering aroma wafted toward them.

"That smells very good," Elodie observed, but Silvanus did not reply.

Elodie had had enough. "Silvanus!" she said in a shrill voice. "If you're not going to say a single word to me, I want you to take me back right now! I don't want to eat with a robot that only knows how to shovel food in its mouth."

She turned and headed back to the car. Silvanus followed her and grabbed her by the arm.

"I'm sorry, Elodie, I just don't know what to say to you. I don't know what you like or what interests you, so I'd rather be quiet than say anything that would upset you."

"And how are you going to find out all these things about me if you don't talk?" she snapped. "Ask me questions and I'll answer, or we can talk about something else. Just say something, at least."

Silvanus stared at her in surprise. "I'm sorry, I didn't

know that my silence upset you so much. Please, let's go in and have some dinner, and I promise I'll talk."

He took her gently by the arm and led her back to the restaurant. Inside, booths lined both walls and two tables stood in the middle. The waitress led them to a booth with a green, white and red striped tablecloth. As soon as they were seated, freshly baked corn tortilla chips and red salsa appeared on the table, together with the menus. They ordered enchiladas with rice and beans and a side of guacamole. It was delicious, and as they ate, Silvanus finally started to talk about himself. He spoke haltingly at first, but with Elodie's encouragement, he opened up and shared with her little details of his life. The evening went by quickly, and after a cup of sugary coffee, Silvanus took care of the check and they left.

Arriving at her place, Elodie said, "Thank you for a lovely dinner and conversation, it was most enjoyable." She kissed him gently on the cheek, then opened her door and quickly went inside without looking back.

Well, who would have thought that Silvanus could be so entertaining? Deep in thought, Elodie donned her nightgown and slipped into her lonely bed.

3

A Disastrous Picnic

FOR THE NEXT FEW weeks, Elodie and Silvanus met regularly for lunch and often went out together on weekends. Their relationship had become comfortable. There was no excitement in it, but at least they were not alone.

One sunny Sunday morning, Silvanus knocked on her door with a huge bouquet of spring flowers in his arms, which he shyly handed to Elodie. "I know we both work in a garden shop, but I thought you might enjoy some colorful flowers to brighten your apartment," he said.

"They're beautiful, thank you so much! Please come in," she replied. She was touched by the gesture but couldn't help thinking that he believed her apartment needed color.

Maybe he was right; it was a bit drab with the old,

scratched furniture she had found at garage sales and swap meets. She had meant to refurbish the pieces of furniture but had never gotten around to it. And over time, she had gotten used to the place and had no longer seen the need to change it.

"I have a cooler with some food and drinks in the car. I thought we might go out walking along the river and have a picnic somewhere along the riverbank."

Elodie nodded in agreement. She grabbed her purse and a light jacket, and off they went. Silvanus drove slowly on the country lanes until they came to a fork in the road. He steered to the left, and soon they came to a meadow bordering the river. He parked under the shade of a huge oak tree. Leaving the picnic basket in the trunk, they walked along a narrow, winding path overhung with old trees. They had not gone far before they found a pleasant, hidden spot with fallen trees that could serve as seats.

"Stay here, Elodie, and I'll fetch the food. I won't be long," he said.

Elodie made herself comfortable and looked out over the river. Water spiders floated on sticks and leaves, gnats and flies buzzed close to the surface and some small birds stopped for a drink. Lilies grew on the riverbank, together with some brush-like flowers that Elodie did not recognize. The sky was a clear blue, and only a few clouds congregated in the west.

"I'm back," Silvanus said gently. He helped Elodie to her feet, and they spread the green-and-blue checkered blanket on the uneven floor and sat down. He handed her a ham-and-cheese sandwich and a glass of wine.

"Thank you," she said, wondering what this was all about.

They ate in silence, and once the paper napkins and plastic glasses were put away, they lay down on the checkered blanket and looked up at the vast sky, where by now a few more clouds had gathered. Silvanus took Elodie's hand and rolled toward her, trying to kiss her on the mouth. Elodie turned away, but Silvanus was insistent.

Oh, well, Elodie thought. *It was bound to happen sooner or later. It's the way of the world, and there's no harm in a little kiss.*

She could not have been more mistaken. Silvanus found her lips, and she was forced to endure his punishing kiss. There was no gentleness in it. He ripped her blouse open and squeezed her nipples in his calloused hands. Elodie shrieked and tried to get his hands off her, but he was too strong. He pulled her skirt up to her waist, unbuttoned his pants and entered her without so much as a caress. Elodie felt searing pain deep inside her as Silvanus convulsed on top of her, crushing her under his weight. With all her strength, she pushed him away.

Feelings of hatred, shame, humiliation and rage pulsated through her body. She propped herself up on one elbow and glared at him with dark, resentful eyes. Silvanus lay peacefully beside her, eyes closed, oblivious to her pain. A contented smile played around his lips.

"Elodie, I've never been with a woman," he whispered. "You're the first." He slowly opened his eyes and looked dreamily at her.

Elodie just had time to avert her eyes so he could not see the hurt in hers. Seeing his expression, she could not bring herself to tell him how she felt. She knew instinctively that he had not meant to hurt her, and he could not have known that she had never been with a man before—although she doubted that would have changed anything. He pulled her back toward him and kissed her again, this time more gently, but his kiss did not stir any feelings in her. It was like a wet cloth on a cold sore.

She remembered one kiss, and one kiss only, so many years ago in Paris, when Hutch had kissed her good-bye at Charles de Gaulle Airport. He had swept her into his arms and parted her waiting lips softly with his tongue, and his last words were etched indelibly on her lips. She could still recall the emotions that had raced through her. A stream of hot lava and ice water had mingled in the pit of her stomach, but before she could speak, Hutch had released her and disappeared into the crowd.

Suddenly, Elodie heard Silvanus ask, "Are you all right? You look as if you had gone far away."

"Please hand me some napkins so I can clean up the mess here." As Silvanus watched with uncomprehending eyes, Elodie silently cleaned the blood stain on the blanket, fashioned a panty liner out of the napkins and pulled up her panties, then got up and straightened her skirt. Finally, she turned toward him and said simply, "I'd never had sex before."

He gasped and took her into his arms. "My darling

Elodie, I had no idea! I just assumed that you must have had many lovers because you're so likeable."

Elodie's only response was to start packing up the picnic items. "Please take me back home. I'm exhausted," she said.

They walked silently back to the car, and Silvanus dropped her off at her apartment. Wearily, Elodie climbed the stairs and entered her apartment. The first thing she saw was the fresh flowers on the table, their bright blooms mocking her. She ripped them out of the crystal vase and violently stuffed them into the garbage can. She took a hot shower with lots of perfumed body wash and put on her favorite flannel pajamas. Then she turned on the television and mindlessly sat in front of it without caring what program was showing. Slowly, painfully, tears began to well up in her eyes, but as usual, Elodie suppressed them and sat staring at the television screen with dry, burning eyes.

4

Silvanus

OVER THE NEXT several weeks, Elodie saw Silvanus only rarely. She tried to keep out of his way and avoid places he frequented. However, one rainy Saturday evening he rang her doorbell. When she opened the door, he handed her a card and motioned her to read it. She nodded and stepped aside to let him in. He silently sat on the dark-brown sofa while she read the card. It was a note apologizing for the disastrous picnic. Silvanus's handwriting was striking, and although he expressed himself awkwardly, Elodie read between the lines and understood his distress and his sincere wish to make amends for his blunder.

Elodie set the card on the coffee table. "Thank you for the genuine apology," she said with a tiny glow on her cheeks. "Let's put that afternoon behind us and look forward."

Silvanus jumped up from the sofa and embraced Elodie. "I never thought I'd hear you say that," he whispered in her ear. "Am I really forgiven for being such a clumsy guy?"

"We all make mistakes," she answered simply.

"Let's go celebrate with a special dinner at a special place!"

"Give me five minutes and I'll be ready to go." Observing that Silvanus was wearing, as usual, his blue jeans and a button-down shirt, she knew that she was dressed adequately in her blue jeans and her colorful T-shirt.

They left five minutes later, and he drove to a well-known restaurant by the riverfront. It was a two-story wooden building with a large terrace where, during the summer, a live band played. The place was full, but they were seated quickly by one of the windows overlooking the river.

"This is a pretty spot," Elodie remarked.

"You've never been here?" Silvanus replied, surprised.

"I don't go out much on my own," she confessed. Looking at her menu, she asked, "Is there anything you especially recommend?"

"Whatever I've eaten here so far has always been very tasty, and the portions are generous," he replied.

"I think I'll have fish-and-chips," Elodie said, "I really like that and haven't had any in quite a while."

The waitress came to take their order, and Silvanus ordered the fish-and-chips for her and the prime rib dinner for himself, along with a bottle of red house wine and some water. Elodie looked pensively out on the river and wondered what this night would bring. Her thoughts were cut short, though, when their dinner arrived, and a huge plate heaped with food was placed in front of Elodie. She gaped at it, then at Silvanus.

"You weren't kidding about the generous portions," she said, laughing, and dug into her food. She had not realized how hungry she was. She had not had breakfast or lunch. The fish was crisp, the French fries freshly made and the wine delicious. They talked about this and that, and before they realized it, their plates were empty and their bellies full.

"Some dessert?" the waitress asked expectantly. They both declined and Silvanus asked for the check. He paid and they left, leaving their seats for the next hungry couple.

When they arrived at Elodie's apartment, she invited him in for a cup of coffee. He accepted, and they climbed the stairs together. Elodie made the coffee while Silvanus checked for a movie they could watch. "Do you have a favorite movie genre?" he asked.

"Not really, it depends on my mood," she called from the kitchen. She brought the coffee and some cookies she had baked earlier in the day, and Silvanus showed her the movies he thought they might watch.

"What about this one?" She pointed to *Forrest Gump*. "It's from the nineties, but it won an Oscar, and I've always liked it."

"Good choice, Elodie."

They settled down on the sofa with the coffee and cookies and watched Tom Hanks as the simpleminded

Forrest Gump. When it was over, Silvanus turned to Elodie and took her in his arms. It felt good to Elodie and she snuggled close to him. Silvanus took this as encouragement; he crushed her to him and pressed his mouth to hers. Elodie gasped for air, laughingly took him by the hand and guided him to her bedroom. She undressed and invited him to do the same. They slipped between the cool sheets, and before Elodie could say a word, he had entered her. Elodie felt a little pain, but nothing she could not deal with. She felt no pleasure, either, but she supposed that this was all there was to lovemaking and that what she had read in novels were just tales. When Silvanus was done with his business, he rolled off her and fell asleep by her side. Elodie tried to think for a while, but the wine took over, and she fell into a dreamless sleep.

Next morning over breakfast, Silvanus surprised her by asking, "What do you think, Elodie, about moving in together? It would be nice to have each other for company, and it would save us some money."

Elodie was taken aback and begged for a little time to think it over. After Silvanus had gone home, Elodie was left to think about his proposition. It was too sudden, but she was tired of being lonely. Maybe he was right—they got along well, and it would be good to have someone to share her life with. The sex was not great, but she knew she could count on him. He would never let her down. It seemed to be a sensible plan.

Later that day, she called him to say that she was agreeable to moving in together. She asked him to come over, as there were many things to figure out, and it would be easier to talk face to face than over the phone. Some twenty minutes later, Silvanus knocked on her door, and they started planning their adventure.

"I was hoping you would move in with me," said Silvanus. "Let's go over to my place so you can see it for yourself."

They drove over to his house, which was located on the other side of town in a small development of about forty houses. Silvanus had bought it some years ago and renovated it. It looked cute with its off-white siding and composite tile roof. A red front door led into the spacious living-dining room, and to the right was a full kitchen with white cabinets and copper cupboard handles. Silvanus had installed dark hardwood flooring throughout the living area, giving the house an air of sophistication. The three bedrooms were in the back of the house, with a small hall bathroom separating the master bedroom from the other two rooms. The honey-colored carpet covering the floors gave the rooms a comfortable air. Silvanus did not have much furniture, and Elodie quickly saw that she could bring the few pieces she owned and make this a home for the two of them.

She turned toward Silvanus, who was watching her anxiously. "This is a very cozy house," she said, "and I'd love to live here with you."

"You would?" Silvanus said happily. "Let's figure out how best to do this."

They sat down on the sofa in the living room and started planning their life, or at least their move-in together. Elodie was somewhat apprehensive about the speed of it all but could not bring herself to shatter Silvanus's happiness. She kept her misgivings to herself. *Who knows?* she thought. *It might turn out better than I can imagine.*

For the next couple of weeks, they were busy arranging for the move. Elodie gave notice at her apartment, and Silvanus arranged for some movers to come and help them. Elodie booked a cleaning service to come and clean after she had moved out. All went well, and before long, Silvanus and Elodie had a common address.

As the months went by, Elodie and Silvanus settled into their daily routine. They worked Monday through Saturday, and on Sundays they went out for breakfast. Evenings were spent in front of the television. Wednesday nights and Sunday mornings, there was sex. Elodie dreaded these minutes but suffered silently through them. To make it bearable, she created a place in her mind that she escaped to whenever Silvanus approached her. Occasionally, they went for a stroll along the river, weather permitting. Elodie sometimes wondered if this was all there was to life—an endless chain of monotonous days.

One Sunday afternoon, a rainstorm was brewing in the west, and Elodie's spirit stirred with a restless longing. "Let's go down to the river and run barefoot along the riverbank," she said to Silvanus. "It will be so much fun!"

But Silvanus glared at her as if she had lost her mind. "Why would you want to do that?" he replied angrily. "The riverbank is slippery and you might fall into the water. And barefoot? Elodie, what are you thinking? You could get stung by insects, or cut your foot on a jagged stone, or maybe even a rusty nail. We're much better off staying at home."

Elodie looked at him in dismay. Without a word, she took her blue cardigan and a blue windbreaker and stormed out of the little house. Silvanus called after her, but the wind swallowed his words, and Elodie marched on. The rain was heavy, and at times she could not see the uneven path in front of her. Periodically she stopped, paused a moment, then continued forward as if she had a destination she needed to reach.

A bus stop appeared ahead of her, and she crossed the field to seek shelter under its glass roof. Sitting on the bench, protected from the rain, she watched the gray sky for any sign of abating rain. She was soaking wet, and from her old shoes little rivulets formed, joining the unruly water in the gutter. Her heart was light, and she was enjoying herself tremendously.

After a while, she felt the cold seeping through her clothes. It was time to return home. She shuddered inwardly at the thought of the boring life that awaited her. Suddenly, she realized that she had to change it. There was no one else who could do it for her. While slowly walking back, she saw her present life like a lonely gray pebble path among dark, sad-looking trees, thick fog silently obscuring what might lie beyond. For a moment, Elodie wondered whether there was anything beyond the trees. Then she saw another path, this one full of colorful neon lights and cheerful music. Happy people were strolling along it, some in large groups and some alone. With sudden clarity, she knew that this was the path she wanted to follow.

By the time, she reached the house, the rain had stopped and her mind was made up. She was going to leave the very next day. She would not tell anybody but just take her things and go.

5

Remembering

ON MONDAY MORNING, she feigned a malaise and told Silvanus to go ahead to the garden center; she would follow in a while. Unsuspecting, Silvanus left, and Elodie prepared for her departure. She took her two old suitcases from the garage and put her belongings into them. She did not have much, and she was done in no time. She had a few mementos and one small painting she wanted to take with her; the rest she did not care about. Then she left a note for Silvanus on the kitchen table and emailed the office to notify them that she would not be returning.

She took one last look at the house where she had lived with Silvanus. Feeling numb, she got behind the wheel of her car and drove away. She had decided to take the interstate to quickly put some distance between her past and her future. Driving along in silence, she let her thoughts wander, and before she realized it, thoughts of Hutch had crept into her mind. She remembered one day in Paris when Hutch had appeared at her door and told her they were going to the South of France for the weekend; he already had the train tickets. She had hurriedly put some clothes into her faded red travel bag, and off they had gone. The memories came flooding back so vividly that she was suddenly back in France, reliving those enchanting days.

଼ଓ

THEY TOOK THE Métro to Paris-Gare de Lyon and boarded a train to Cannes. After a five-hour journey, they arrived late in the afternoon. Hutch had made reservations at a classic old hotel right across from the Château de la Castre, not even a mile away from the seaside Boulevard de la Croisette. They rode the small two-person elevator to the third floor, and when they arrived at their room, Elodie was surprised to see that it had a view of the Mediterranean Sea. It was a small but comfortable room with a queen-sized bed covered by a gray silk comforter, with several pillows in the same color leaning against a headboard upholstered in burgundy satin. Its most astonishing aspect, though, was the twelve-foot ceiling, from which a ceiling fan hung low into the room, humming a contented melody. The windows were the old-fashioned type, narrow and hard to open, with white sheers and dark gray curtains on either side.

Elodie inspected the bathroom and was taken aback

by its appearance. The tops of the walls were tiled with two rows of indigo-colored tiles; beneath them, honey-colored tiles ran down to the bathtub rim. The side of the bathtub was also tiled in that hideous indigo. Even the vanity was tiled in both colors, with a dark-blue countertop and a light-blue wooden door below the sink. The faucets seemed to stem from their grandparents' era, and there was no room for any toiletries. Elodie laughed out loud, and Hutch came to see what had made her laugh.

"What's so funny in here?" he asked.

"Just look at this bathroom! Have you ever seen such color combinations in a bathroom?"

"Actually, yes. The place I rent in Paris looks very similar. It must have been the fashion at one time, long ago."

Elodie shook her head in amusement and closed the door.

"Let's go and explore the town," Hutch suggested. Only a few steps from the hotel, they crossed over a bridge and found themselves in the old part of Cannes. They walked down the narrow, winding cobblestone streets and soon arrived at the harbor. Huge white yachts, resembling castles, were anchored side by side, and Hutch looked at them dreamily.

"One day," he mused, "I'll own a yacht like this."

They strolled on and reached a little plaza close to the Palais des Festivals, where people sat drinking afternoon aperitifs. When they spotted a free table, they sat down and ordered pastis and appetizers.

"These little tarts make me hungry," Hutch said.

"Me, too," Elodie agreed. "Maybe we could have dinner in one of the little bistros we saw on our way here," she volunteered.

"Good idea. Let's finish up here and then find a place that serves early dinner."

They had retraced their steps and had soon found a little restaurant offering outdoor seating. A look at the menu convinced them that they had discovered the perfect place to enjoy the evening. The night was balmy, and they lingered over their meal, savoring their fried calamari, mixed salad and bottle of white house wine. The food was delicious, and the wine was light and went down smoothly.

"You okay?" Hutch had asked after a while. "You look awfully tired."

"I am tired. If you don't mind, I'd like to go back to the hotel and sleep."

"Fine with me. We have a whole day tomorrow to investigate the city and its sights."

They stood up and walked slowly up the hill toward their hotel. When they entered the lobby, the bar was in full swing, and Hutch looked longingly at it.

"Go have a drink before you come upstairs," Elodie said.

"I think I will. See you later."

He entered the bar, and Elodie took the elevator to their floor. She hurriedly got ready for bed, and soon she was fast asleep.

In the morning, the smell of freshly baked bread woke her up. The sun was already high in the sky, and Hutch was sleeping peacefully beside her. She quietly got up and showered. When she came out, he was watching television.

"It got a bit late yesterday." He grinned sheepishly at her. "The smell of breakfast makes me hungry."

"I'll go downstairs and have a cup of coffee while you get ready."

"Sounds good, see you in a little bit."

Elodie went downstairs and found that breakfast was being served in the garden. She chose a table by an old tree at the edge of the deck and sat down with her cup of coffee. Soon, Hutch joined her, and they had a lovely breakfast of freshly baked croissants, brioche, baguettes and French bread with butter, jam, and a variety of cheeses and cold cuts, accompanied by lots of strong black coffee.

"Where would you like to go today?" Hutch asked.

"I'll follow you. I have no clue what one is supposed to do or see in Cannes."

"Okay, I have a few ideas. Let's go and look at the castle across from here."

They ascended the steps to the Château de la Castre. The view of old town and the marina was breathtaking, and they strolled around the gardens for a while. Then they descended toward the marina on a narrow, winding path and found themselves again by the harbor. The street was lined with stately old buildings in hues of ginger, sand and white, with little balconies jutting out from the top floors. The shutters were mostly a soft green that complemented the façades perfectly.

Soon, they came to an outdoor market. Elodie was

charmed by a little painting she spotted in one of the stalls, depicting a crooked little house sitting among blooming flowers overlooking a meadow. She exclaimed, "What a precious little picture! It reminds me of a grandma's house, or what I think a grandma's house should look like."

"It looks kind of old," Hutch replied, "but if you like it, buy it."

Elodie took only a moment before she decided to purchase it as a memento of this weekend.

A little further up the street, they came to the Marché Forville, a covered market with fruit, vegetables, meat and fish for sale. Along the street behind it were restaurants serving a variety of appetizers, drinks, and full dinners.

With so much to see, the day passed quickly, and they were both tired and hungry. They decided to walk along the water's edge and see if they could find a restaurant to their liking. A quaint Moroccan restaurant attracted their attention, and when they entered, an exotic scene met their eyes: low benches and chairs scattered with colorful pillows, imaginary windows covered with thick silk curtains and walls hung with paintings of desert landscapes, oases and beautiful belly dancers. After a delicious meal of couscous with lamb, they walked back to the hotel and had a drink at the bar, then went up to their room.

Elodie's mind was a crazy mixture of fear and hope. Would Hutch try to make love to her? Would he be gentle? Or would he be rough? She had read accounts of passionate lovemaking that made the world seem to stand still, but also horrific stories of violence. Nothing happened between them, though. They watched television for a few minutes until Hutch fell asleep. Elodie didn't know whether to feel relieved or disappointed. Did Hutch not find her attractive enough?

Next morning, Hutch was his usual self. Elodie felt confused but took the lead from him and behaved as if nothing were amiss. After again having breakfast outside in the garden, they checked out and walked to the train station. By mid-afternoon, they were back in Paris, and each went their separate way to their lodgings.

6

Toward a New Life

ELODIE HEADED EAST on Interstate 80, driving toward a new life. When the daylight started to fade, she pulled into the parking lot of a motel and stayed the night. Early the next morning, she drove on toward Mount Rushmore. She had always wanted to see the faces of the four presidents, but Silvanus had never wanted to go there. Now, she took the road toward the famous monument.

She was awed by the sight. There they were: George Washington, Thomas Jefferson, Abraham Lincoln and Theodore Roosevelt, their stern faces hewn into the granite overlooking the Black Hills of South Dakota. Gazing up at these well-known faces, Elodie wondered what these men would think of what their America had become. Her thoughts were interrupted by a loud thunderclap, and she walked back to her car as the first raindrops started to fall. She drove on through Badlands National Park. The stone formations along the road were spectacular, exposing narrow canyons, tall pinnacles and slender spires in an array of colors ranging from chocolate brown to terra-cotta to burnished gold. Elodie enjoyed the view enormously. The striking geography reminded her of an earlier time, and her thoughts wandered off again, taking her back to her childhood.

She was in the meadow where the children of her village used to play. That afternoon, there had been huge white clouds in the sky, and they had lain down on the warm grass and stared up at the clouds, waiting for recognizable forms to appear. This had been one of Elodie's favorite games. There were rabbits, old men's faces, strange, beautiful flowers and scary, mythical figures. She would often connect the images in her mind by making up stories about them. She could have happily stayed there all afternoon, but all too soon, the other children had gotten bored and left. Not wanting to stay behind, Elodie, with a heavy heart, had followed them back to the village. It had been time to go home, anyway.

A shrill sound tore through the silence, and Elodie wrested her mind back to the present and concentrated on the road. Traffic had grown heavier, and as some drivers were dawdling in the left lane, refusing to move to the right to make way for faster cars, her progress was slow. Elodie fumed at these drivers who so self-righteously stayed in the left lane without any consideration for their fellow drivers. *I bet they must be awful people, hard to please and always right,* she thought.

Traffic started to ease again, and Elodie's thoughts fixed on a subject she had avoided until now: Silvanus and Hutch. She compared the only two men she had ever had feelings for. Hutch was the easygoing, happy-go-lucky type, whereas Silvanus was the cautious one, slow to decide anything and never attempting anything spontaneously. She did not want to judge him, but she had to admit that he was boring and very much set in his ways. Even though he was the same age as Hutch, he seemed to be years older. Life with him would have been a chain of interminably gray days. She suspected that with Hutch, life would be a loud, colorful party. But then, she did not know. She allowed herself the luxury of imagining being with Hutch. Her reverie was interrupted, however, when she approached a busy intersection, and her attention focused on the road once again.

Soon, the sun set on the endless plain, and Elodie stopped at a small hotel where she got a room. That night, she dreamed of being in a big, old house with both Hutch and Silvanus, each of them vying for her favor. She could not make up her mind until Silvanus left them for a few minutes and she found herself alone with Hutch. He gently took her arm, and a feeling of intense pleasure and tormenting yearning engulfed her. She was ready, waiting for Hutch to touch her, when she awakened. Painfully, she realized that it had been but a dream, and she was alone in a hotel by the road. She was unable to go back to sleep, and early in the morning she drove on.

She got off the highway and took surface roads for a while, eager to see something of this enormous country that she called home. At the entrance to a village, whose name she did not know, she bought a sandwich, then pulled into the parking lot of a general store—or at least, that's what she thought it was. When she inspected it more closely, however, she realized that it was a nursery with a florist shop. On impulse, she got out of the car and pushed open the glass doors to go inside. She was amazed at what she saw; the store was huge, with a floral section where women were busily making flower arrangements, and an extensive gift section with all types of garden accessories, thoughtful and fun gifts for gardeners of every ilk.

"Are you looking for something for a special occasion?" a warm voice asked her. Elodie turned around and looked into the face of an older woman with a broad smile on her pleasant face.

"I was just looking around," she said. "This is a beautiful store. I used to work in a flower store in California, but it was nothing compared to this. It must be delightful to work here among all these lovely things."

"Thank you for the compliment. I do like working here." The woman smiled. "I should, I own the store."

Elodie, seized by a sudden whim, blurted out, "By any chance, do you have an opening for someone like me?"

"Are you serious?"

"Very much so."

As it turned out, there was an opening in the floral department. One of the employees had gotten married a year ago, and with a second baby on the way, she had decided to stay home.

"I'm Heather Brown," said the woman. "Come, I'll show you around, and we can get acquainted with each other."

She gave Elodie the grand tour of the property, then showed her where she would be working. It was a small space behind the flower boutique, where all types of flowers rested in big buckets, impatiently waiting to be picked and hoping to be the star of the bouquet. Elodie saw immediately that these were quality flowers and that it would be a pleasure to work here. She could already picture herself behind the green table, cutting and arranging flowers into lovely works of art.

"Do you feel up to creating something for me?"

"I would love to," replied Elodie and selected a vase. She filled it with pink roses, white peonies, pink tulips and one pink hydrangea, a white orchid and a white snapdragon, then completed the arrangement with some variegated ivy and green, shiny-leaved stems. She stepped back from the table.

"This is fabulous!" Heather exclaimed. "If you want it, the job is yours."

"When do I start?" asked Elodie with a smile.

"Come, let's go to my office and get everything sorted out."

She led Elodie through a long, narrow corridor to her office in the back of the store. Two huge windows looked out over the fields. A dark, gleaming wooden table served as a desk, with a matching cupboard and a comfortable brown leather chair behind. Heather motioned to Elodie to sit on an olive-green, satin-covered bench. While she was taking out the paperwork, Elodie peered around the space, liking what she saw. Three walls of the room were painted a milk-coffee color. The fourth was divided into three horizontal panels, the middle one painted in the same milk-coffee color as the other walls, framed by panels painted in a darker shade of coffee. Ebony-colored wainscoting divided light from dark, and several pictures hanging in the center space gave the room a sophisticated appearance. In the opposite corner stood a dark-red-and-beige sofa with an ottoman that could serve as a coffee table. A tall glass lamp filled the room with a warm light.

"My husband and I took over this store many years ago," Heather said, "and it has grown over time. I'll tell you all about it later. For now, we need to get the paperwork started."

She pushed some papers toward Elodie and asked her to fill them out. When Elodie hesitated, she asked, "Is something wrong?"

"No," replied Elodie, "only I don't have an address here yet. I've been driving for several days and just arrived here from the West Coast. I haven't had a chance to find a place to live."

Heather took the papers back and studied them. "Elodie, what a beautiful name. I tell you what; there's a little inn not far from here where you can stay for a few days. They have good prices. You'll find an apartment in this village without too much searching. Once you have an address, we can complete the paperwork."

She wrote down the name of the inn, and Elodie left

to find the place and check the newspaper for any apartments to be let.

The inn turned out to be a quaint brick house nestled among pine trees. Heather had called ahead, and when Elodie rang the doorbell, the innkeeper opened the door and welcomed her inside.

"You look tired," she said. "I'll take you to your room. If there's anything you need, just ask."

The innkeeper climbed the stairs ahead of Elodie, opened the door to a friendly room, and handed her the newspaper. Elodie thanked her and sat down in the chair by the window, exhausted. She was too tired to unpack; all she wanted was to go to sleep.

"But I must unpack. I have to be at work tomorrow," she scolded herself in a firm voice to push herself into action. She hung some clothes in the wardrobe and rummaged through her traveling bag for some granola bars and a bottle of water.

"This will do for tonight," she mumbled to herself. She put on her pajamas, slid between the sheets and was sound asleep before her head hit the pillow.

7

The Flower Store

THE ALARM CLOCK shrilled, and Elodie woke up with
a start. It took her a few moments to gather her
thoughts and figure out where she was. Then it all
came back to her. She had stopped somewhere to buy a
sandwich and had eaten it in the parking lot of a flower
store.

"I met this woman, Heather something," she
muttered to herself, "and she offered me a job. I think I
said I was going to be there this morning."

A glance at her phone told her that it was already
7:30 a.m. Elodie took a quick shower, dressed in jeans
and a steel-blue T-shirt and went downstairs. She was
just about to open the front door when she heard a
friendly voice.

"Good morning, Elodie. Did you sleep well?"

"Oh," Elodie stammered, "I didn't see you. Yes, I

slept very well, thank you. I'm off to the flower store to see if Heather really wants to hire me."

"Wait a moment," the innkeeper replied, smiling. "Breakfast is served, and you need something in your belly if you're going to work for Heather."

"But I'm already a bit late," she countered.

"Don't worry! Heather and I are old friends, and I've already talked to her this morning. She reminded me to make sure you had some hearty breakfast before going over there."

"I could do with a cup of coffee and some toast," Elodie admitted, and she followed the innkeeper to the breakfast room. It was a sunny, pleasant room with stained glass windows, wallpaper with teal and red flowers and dark-brown wainscoting like that in Heather's office. The tables were arranged beautifully around the room, and the table linens matched the wall colors. Elodie spotted a table set for one in the corner by the window and looked inquiringly at the innkeeper, who nodded.

"I thought you might like to enjoy the flowers and sunshine. It's not every day that the weather is so benign."

Elodie sat down and inspected the fine white porcelain cup and saucer set on the table. When her breakfast arrived—a poached egg with hollandaise sauce on a bed of spinach, a small fried tomato, mushrooms and country fried potatoes and a little handmade basket of buttered toast, along with hot, steaming coffee—Elodie suddenly realized that she was quite hungry. With a smile, she helped herself to the homemade boysenberry jam and heartily cut into the perfectly cooked poached egg. When she was full, she pushed the rattan chair back and got up. The innkeeper opened the door for her and wished her a good day.

In a good mood, Elodie drove to the flower shop. As she was walking toward the entrance, Heather spotted her and waved.

"Come this way, and I'll introduce you to the team." Elodie followed her to what seemed to be a meeting room, where several women were drinking coffee.

"This is Elodie," Heather announced. "I hired her yesterday, and I hope she will stay with us for a while."

After the introduction, they went back to Heather's office once again to complete Elodie's paperwork.

"Did you have a good breakfast?" Heather asked.

"Oh, yes," Elodie replied. "It was delicious."

"The room was okay?"

"Very nice and cozy, and I slept very well."

"Wonderful!" She handed Elodie some papers. "Please fill out these forms—they're required by the city—while I look through my mail."

While Elodie filled out the papers, Heather looked on. After a minute, she asked casually, "What brings you out here? It's a long way from California."

Elodie glanced up to see Heather studying her curiously.

"I wanted to see more of the country and live somewhere else for a while. As far as I can see, this is as good a place as any," she answered, a slightly defensive note creeping into her voice.

Heather seemed amused. "I didn't mean to pry; I just

like to get to know my employees a little." She dropped the subject, much to Elodie's relief.

When Elodie had finished filling out the forms, she pushed them toward Heather.

"Your name is Elodie Thorn? Like in the novel *The Thorn Birds?*" Heather asked.

"Yes," Elodie answered. "I'm familiar with the story, but I've never read the book myself, nor seen the miniseries."

"I used to wait impatiently for each episode. I really, really liked Richard Chamberlain." Heather exhaled with a long sigh of contentment.

The conversation returned to business matters, and they discussed salary, days off, work shifts and benefits. Heather explained in detail what she expected of Elodie and afterwards led her to her new workstation in the little room behind the flower shop.

"We usually do not create many arrangements in advance, as we prefer to make them to the customer's wishes. However, maybe we should have a few generic ones on display for customers who would rather buy an arrangement than a bunch of flowers. What do you think?"

"That's a good idea. In the flower shop where I used to work, we usually had a few on display before the holidays to give customers an idea of what kind of arrangements they might like."

"Please make about five arrangements you think would be customer favorites, and we'll put them on display and see how it goes," Heather replied, and she left the room.

Alone in the little room, Elodie carefully looked the flowers over and selected a few vases and containers to use for her arrangements. Soon, customers began arriving, and Elodie was asked to help with putting bouquets together. Observing that the other employees gave the customers exactly what they asked for, Elodie did the same, closely following the customers' instructions. But often, she would have liked to add or omit some flowers. The day passed in a blur, and when it was closing time, Elodie swept the floor, put the unused vases back on the shelf and poured fresh water into the buckets of flowers.

Heather came in to lock up and was pleased to see that the workroom was already clean and ready for tomorrow.

"So, how was your day?" she inquired, and Elodie's eyes brightened.

"Marvelous! People in this part of the country are so friendly, and it's a pleasure to deal with them. I've made a couple of arrangements for tomorrow and put them into buckets with fresh water. They'll easily last for a few days."

Elodie took her coat from the rack, wished Heather a good evening and left the store.

☙

HEATHER WATCHED her new employee walk away, then turned back to inspect the arrangements that Elodie had created. They were so intriguing—the colors matched one another beautifully, but there was a longing in them that belied Elodie's outwardly sunny disposition. The arrangements hinted at untold stories and hidden mysteries.

She's a quiet one, full of emotions that have no way out, she thought to herself. She hoped in time she would be able to penetrate the thick armor that surrounded Elodie and get to know her better. In the meantime, she would watch her closely. Eventually, she might let her guard down and find solace by confiding her troubles.

Heather turned and went upstairs to her apartment, still deep in thought.

8

An Evening with Heather

ELODIE FOUND A small apartment close to work and settled in. As the weeks passed, she bought some furniture at a flea market and restored an old table and four dining chairs to their former glory. She was quite pleased with the outcome, and whenever time and weather permitted, she roamed from garage sale to estate sale or scoured the flea markets in the neighboring towns. She usually came home with her arms full of treasures that needed to be cleaned, polished or painted. She enjoyed working with her hands, and the time flew by.

The days grew shorter, and soon the weather turned cold. The autumn mornings had a chill in the air that dissipated as the midday sun warmed the world. As December approached, however, the sun turned a wintry white, and the trees started to lose their colorful leaves. It was a beautiful time of the year, and Elodie found herself making arrangements that mimicked the season. Customers at the store loved her designs, and Elodie was in great demand. She had made a few friends, and sometimes she went with them to a movie and dinner, or even the occasional all-day outing. She was content with her life, yet somewhere in the back of her mind, she felt that something was missing.

One evening, after Elodie had just finished cleaning up her worktable, Heather strolled in. "Do you have anything planned for tonight?" she asked.

"No," Elodie replied, looking questioningly at Heather.

"Come with me, and we can talk while we have dinner. I've ordered some takeout, and I'm sure you will approve of it."

She led the way toward her office, from which a door opened onto narrow stairs that led up to her second-floor apartment. Elodie was amazed at the spacious-ness of the living area and was still scanning the room when Heather invited her to sit down at a beautifully set table. White dishes were placed on dusky-red placemats framed by matching napkins; the cutlery was delicately made, and Elodie wondered whether they were a family heirloom. The long-stemmed wine glasses reflected the dimmed lights, and the whole room was bathed in a warm glow. Heather brought in the food, and the smell made Elodie realize that she was hungry. She helped herself to creamy mashed potatoes, buttery rabbit stew and green string beans.

"Hungry?" asked Heather.

"I am," she answered. "I didn't have lunch; there was too much to do. But all is ready now for the wedding tomorrow."

"I appreciate your efforts. I've been thinking, I'd like you to be my backup when I'm not at the shop so the employees know whom they can talk to should there be any issues. What do you think? Do you want to take on that extra responsibility? Of course, you'll be compensated accordingly."

Elodie was stunned. She had never expected this; she had only worked here for a few months. But she would gladly accept the challenge and told Heather so.

"Let's drink to our new work relationship," Heather said, and they lifted their glasses.

After dinner, they retired to the cozy sitting room, where a fire was burning in the fireplace, spreading warmth throughout the room. Heather elaborated further on her plans for Elodie and the shop. Elodie tried to focus on what Heather was saying, but exhausted from her day, she dozed off for a minute. When she opened her eyes, Heather was returning from the kitchen with a tray of steaming coffee and cookies.

"Had a good snooze?" Heather laughingly asked.

"I'm sorry about that. The food was delicious and the place is nice and warm. I couldn't help myself."

"No harm done. I made some coffee; would you like a cup?"

"Yes, please."

They silently sipped coffee, and Heather started to tell Elodie how she and her husband had acquired the flower shop. She had grown up in rural Illinois in a family of seven children. Theirs had been a happy childhood without drama or hardship. They had enjoyed the hot summers splashing in the river and playing in the snow during the harsh winters. She had married her high school sweetheart, Frederik. He had had a good job at the mill and had assumed he would work there his whole life, as his father had. Then one day, her husband had come home and told her that he had lost his job. They were downsizing, and he had been one of the casualties. He had taken it very hard, and it had been tough for Heather to see him suffering without being able to alleviate his despair.

As the weeks had passed and no job offers had come along, Frederik had decided to search further afield. One evening, he had come home excited about a little flower shop that was for sale in the neighboring village. He had always liked the idea of owning his own business, and a garden shop seemed to be the perfect match for him. It reminded him of his grandmother's garden and the joy she had derived from planting seedlings and watching them grow. He had already talked to the owner to get all the details; he had told the man he was interested but needed to discuss the decision with his wife. Heather did not know what to think or say. She had been stunned, and her first impulse had been to say no. But when she had seen the light sparkle in Frederik's eyes, she had known that she could never crush his hopes with a simple no.

"Let's look at the proposal and see if we can do this," she had said.

"You mean it? Really?" Frederik had replied eagerly.

Together, they had poured over the proposal, the payment terms and what it would entail to embark on such an adventure. The next day, they had driven to the flower shop, and Heather had met the owner, a short, stocky man in his seventies with thinning white hair and a hunched back. He had been wearing black shoes a couple of sizes too big for his small feet, making it seem as if he were sliding rather than walking on the floor. His handshake had been firm, however, belying his weak appearance. He had shown them around the property—Heather could see that it had a lot of potential—and had told them that his wife had passed away some years ago, and without her help, the shop had become too much for him to run alone. His children had left the village years ago to live in the big city and were not interested in taking over the shop.

"You two are young and strong, and you can make this into a lovely store if you don't mind the work," he had said to them. "My wife and I had big plans, but then the children came along, and she had to split her time between them and the store. We had planned to expand and build a greenhouse in the back, but we never got the chance. Now it's too late for me, but you can make it your dream."

He had led them back to his cramped office, and they had signed the paperwork. They had agreed to pay him a small down payment, and then as much as they could every month. "In those days, people trusted one another." Heather sighed.

Elodie nodded in agreement, and Heather continued with her story.

Frederik and Heather had moved into the small space behind the store and had started to work on expanding the plant-growing space while selling flowers to the villagers. Soon they had realized that they needed more than just flowers and had built the greenhouse. They had tried growing vegetables from seeds and selling the little plants, and their experiment had been an instant success. Almost every house in the village had a vegetable garden, and people were happy to buy the seedlings rather than grow them from seeds themselves. Heather had been able to hire help to do the heavy work, and she had devoted more and more time to the flower arrangements.

As word had spread of the improvements they were making, the store had prospered, and they had eventually added the upstairs floor that became their apartment. Some time later, they had enlarged the store and had started to sell potted plants, pots and garden accessories such as potting soil, fertilizer, garden hoses, shovels, rakes and a variety of specialized gardening tools. A few years before Frederik's death, they had added the gift section and stocked it with whimsical garden statues, bird baths in different styles, colorful stepping stones, small potted plants that made thoughtful gifts, and even hats and T-shirts.

"You see, the store has been like this now for many years, and it always reminds me of my Frederik and the joy he derived from owning this place," Heather said, tears welling up in her dark-blue eyes. She quickly wiped them off with the back of her hand, and a flash of wild grief darted over her face.

Elodie decided that it was time for her to go. She got up and said, "Thank you so much for a wonderful evening."

"I hope this isn't the last time we can sit and chat together," Heather replied.

Together, they went downstairs. Elodie said good-bye and walked briskly back to her apartment. Her head was spinning with Heather's story, and she wondered why Heather had chosen her to look after the store in her absence.

Eventually it will all make sense, she thought as she entered her apartment.

9

The Break-In

ELODIE WAS SO BUSY at the store that she hardly noticed when Thanksgiving and Christmas came and went, giving way to especially harsh winter weather in the new year. Sometimes she went to the movies with one of the other women who worked at the store, but even though she enjoyed the snow, she was not used to going out in the bitter cold and preferred to spend most of her evenings at home in the company of a good book. She sometimes worked late with Heather, making plans to add more merchandise to the store in the spring. Heather gave Elodie increasingly greater responsibility and put her in charge of finding the items at the best prices possible. Elodie's knowledge of suppliers that had delivered goods to the West Coast store came in handy, and she was able to conclude some good deals for Heather.

Slowly, winter relinquished its hold on the countryside, and the days became warmer. The next few months passed without incident, and suddenly, summer was just around the corner with its humid heat and long daylight hours that lingered well into the evening. Elodie had settled into a daily routine, getting up early in the morning, making herself a cup of steaming black coffee, and eating her breakfast—either cereal, or toast with jam and cheese—while reading a newspaper on her tablet. She had downloaded newspapers from several countries and enjoyed reading different accounts of the same events.

One morning, after loading her dishes in the dishwasher, she left for the garden shop. The walk was pleasant; the sun was shining and the trees were green and laden with fruit. Soon it would be harvesttime.

When Elodie opened the door to the shop, she was surprised to see Heather with two uniformed police officers. Heather motioned her over.

"There was a break-in during the night, and the cash register has been pried open. Most of the flowers were left alone, but many of your arrangements were smashed to the floor. I just can't imagine why anyone would want to do such a thing."

Heather was in tears, and Elodie put her arms around her.

"Come and sit down, and I'll talk to the officers."

There had been several break-ins in the neighborhood during the past few weeks, and the police had a good idea who was behind it, but they needed proof. The three of them went into Elodie's workshop and searched the premises for evidence.

"I don't believe this," one of the officers exclaimed. "Here's a cell phone." With his gloved hand, he fished it out from under the table and held it up to the light. He carefully put it into a plastic bag and turned to Elodie with a big grin on his face.

"If this doesn't belong to any of the employees, we have a good chance of identifying the owner and the thief," he said. "We will contact you as soon as we know."

The officers took their leave and drove off in their black-and-white cruiser. Elodie went to apprise Heather of the discovery and found her sitting in her office, looking at Frederik's picture.

"The police found a cell phone under the table, and they believe it might belong to the thief. As soon as they know, they'll contact us."

Heather put the picture on her lap and looked sadly at Elodie. "How could anybody destroy such beautiful arrangements? They're made to bring people joy with their innocent blooms," she whispered.

"Come, I'll take you upstairs. I'll deal with the staff, and tomorrow you'll feel better. Maybe you could consider a security system for the shop?" Elodie suggested. Heather nodded and sank into the comfortable big chair by the window.

Elodie left her and slowly descended the wooden stairs. There had been a similar incident at the nursery where she used to work, and it had turned out to be a staff member who had committed the crime. The employee had been incensed that a promotion had been given to somebody else and had retaliated by smashing all the flower arrangements and pots, as well as most of the windows. The perpetrator had been quickly identified and sent to prison for a few years. Elodie wondered whether any of the staff here resented her own promotion to that extent.

Back at the shop, she called a meeting and informed the staff of the break-in. She watched their reactions to the news and was not surprised that one of them seemed rather sullen. It was a middle-aged woman, Greta, who had worked in the shop for many years and had been a great help to Heather when her husband had passed away. Elodie had felt her resentment from the first day Heather had hired her but had chosen to ignore it. She had learned long ago that some people could be unkind or even outright nasty, especially when nobody else was around, and had tried to avoid being alone with Greta as much as possible.

For the next couple of hours, they cleaned up the store, replacing the broken pots with new ones from the inventory, sorting the flowers and making new arrangements. When they were finished, the shop looked as if nothing had happened, and Elodie thanked everyone for their help.

"I'll go upstairs and see how Heather is doing," she said. "If you need me, please call or text me."

She could almost feel Greta's Nordic blue eyes boring into her back.

She almost seems to hate me, yet she doesn't know me at all, Elodie thought as she strode up the stairs. Once at Heather's door, she hesitated before going in. *I musn't burden Heather with my suspicions. For all I know, it's nothing.*

She knocked, and after a brief moment, Heather called her in. She was still sitting in the same chair where Elodie had left her a couple of hours ago. Her face looked worn, her brow creased with worry, and she stared blankly at Elodie with her mouth open. Elodie pulled one of the side chairs closer and sat down.

"We've cleaned up the store, replaced the broken pots and made up new arrangements. It looks like nothing ever happened," Elodie said, smiling.

"You know that it was Greta who did this, don't you?" Heather asked. "I didn't realize it at first, but then it dawned on me."

Elodie was taken aback at Heather's perception. How could she know? Had Greta's hostility and her own avoidance of Greta been so obvious?

"What makes you say that?" she asked cautiously.

"Your arrangements were the target," Heather said. "The damage to the rest of the store was minor. I've seen the way Greta looks at you when she thinks nobody is watching; she's jealous of you. But I never thought she would vandalize the store.

"It's a long story—it started long before I met Frederik. He and Greta knew each other as children, you see. Both their families came from the same part of Norway. Their great-grandfathers emigrated to America and settled in Door County, in Wisconsin. I believe they had farms around Egg Harbor or Sturgeon Bay. I don't remember.

"Anyhow, as a young girl, Frederik's mother moved

to Illinois. She met her husband there, and they had married and had children. She never went back to Door County, and her relationship with her relatives deteriorated.

"Not long after we bought the shop, Greta came to visit. Somehow, the news that Frederik owned a flower shop had found its way to Door County. So, there she was: good old Greta, with her rosy cheeks and yellow hair as pale as a field of grain, her plump body filling the door frame. She introduced herself as a cousin from Door County, and we invited her in for lunch. We talked—or rather, they talked—about their shared history, people they both might know from the old country.

"I had been busy with the shop while they were reminiscing, but when it was time to close, I had to tell Greta that we didn't have a room for her to stay in—we lived in the spare office in back of the store then, and there was barely room for the two of us. I still remember her look of total surprise; she hadn't realized that we were married. It was terribly awkward, but when Frederik came to my rescue and told her, the color drained from her face, and she shook her head in utter disbelief. I could tell she had had designs on Frederik; maybe she wanted to marry him herself. I haven't a clue why, they had not seen one another in a few years."

"Anyhow, as her plans didn't work out, she left, but over the years, she occasionally came back for a visit. One time, she was very distraught over a lost love and did not want to return to Door County, so Frederik offered her a job. Our little store had grown quite a bit by then, and we needed some help. She agreed to work with us during our busy season, and when Frederik died, I asked her to stay on permanently, and she's been with me ever since. We've kept each other company; she was lonely in Door County, just as I was lonely here, and we had our love for Frederik in common.

"I know she assumed that she was second in command here, but she isn't cut out for that. She takes everything very personally, and I feared she would run the store into the ground with her overpowering personality. Customers don't appreciate being talked back to or having their wishes defied."

She sighed and took Elodie's hand. "I have to let her go. I no longer trust her, and I can't afford for her to chase you away. Please keep this conversation to yourself, though."

"What about the police?"

"There's no need for them to know. I won't press charges as the damage is limited."

"As you wish," Elodie replied, then got up and walked back downstairs.

The rest of the day dragged, and Elodie was glad when she could go home to her cozy apartment.

The next morning, Heather told the staff that Greta had left for personal reasons and was returning to Wisconsin. Nobody seemed to be sad about the news, nor did they ask any questions. Elodie had the feeling that Greta had not been liked by the employees.

That afternoon, one of the police officers came in with the cell phone. It belonged to one of the shop employees, who had been taken ill a few days ago. He asked Heather whether she wanted to press charges if they were able to apprehend the perpetrator, but she declined.

"There wasn't much damage done once the store was cleaned up, and I don't want to waste your time or mine," she said, and the police officer left.

Later in the week, Elodie bumped into the officer while shopping at the farmers' market.

"Your boss is pretty adamant about not filing charges, isn't she?" he asked her.

"She doesn't want the hassle, and there really wasn't much damage. A few broken pots and some trampled flowers."

"Does she suspect anyone?"

"I couldn't say," Elodie replied. "I'm not in her confidence."

She turned away and made to leave, but he grabbed her by the sleeve.

"Don't go yet," he wheedled. "Have a cup of coffee with me at the Corner Bakery. It's much nicer drinking in company than alone."

Elodie wanted to tell him to let go of her arm and go have his stupid coffee by himself. However, when she turned around and saw his disarming smile, her annoyance dissolved and she agreed, amused. They walked over to the café and found a table near the back. They ordered coffee, and he started to talk a bit about himself.

Adam had grown up in a neighboring village, and after he had graduated from the police academy had found a job here. He liked the village with its friendly people and the amenities it offered, and best of all, he was still very close to his family. He lived near the post office in a small house that had belonged to his aunt. After she had passed away, he had been able to buy it inexpensively. He invited Elodie to come and see it, but she declined, feigning an important errand she had to take care of.

"Maybe another day, then?" he asked hopefully.

Elodie nodded vaguely, thanked him for the coffee and left.

"That's the second man I've met who lives in a little house and wants to invite me to see it!" she murmured to herself. Thoughts of Silvanus came blasting back, and she hurried home to hide from the unpleasant memories.

10

A Body in the River

ONE AFTERNOON, on a gorgeous fall day, two police detectives came to the flower store. They showed their badges to Elodie and asked for Heather Brown. She wanted to ask them what this was all about, but their stern, tight-lipped faces dissuaded her from questioning them. She quickly went to the back room and told Heather about the visitors.

"Do you know what they want?" she asked Heather.

"I have my suspicions, but let's wait and see what it is they've come for. Please bring them to the back office and make sure nobody interrupts us."

Elodie was intrigued but followed Heather's instructions. She showed the detectives the way and softly closed the door behind them.

After what seemed to Elodie like hours, the detectives reappeared and left the store, still unsmiling.

Elodie almost ran to Heather's office and was taken aback when she encountered Heather slumped in her chair, her face drained of color and a sad, faraway look in her eyes.

Elodie knelt beside the chair and asked, "What happened? Why did they come?"

Slowly, Heather turned her head and tried to focus on Elodie. "They found a body in the Des Plaines River. A woman's body. She drowned weeks ago and has only just now surfaced. She was badly decomposed, but an autopsy revealed that she must have been poisoned before she hit the water."

"But why did they come to you?"

"It was Greta Hendricksen."

Elodie gasped and took Heather's hand. "They can't think you had something to do with this?"

"I don't think so. They're just following every lead and wanted to know when she had last worked here. As she left months ago, they figured that this is just another piece of the puzzle. But who would want her dead? She was an imposing woman and not always very nice, but killing her?"

Heather fell silent, and Elodie sat down on a chair nearby. Her thoughts swirled in her head as she tried to absorb this terrible news. Sure, she had not much liked Greta, either, but she hadn't deserved to be murdered. Unless there had been more to Greta than they knew.

"Will they come back?" she asked.

"I don't know," Heather answered.

"I'll go downstairs and lock up. Do you want me to

come and keep you company for a while?"

"Yes, please do," Heather said, a grateful smile spreading over her face.

Elodie went downstairs and closed the shop, put all the flowers into their buckets, swept the floor and returned to Heather's apartment.

A fire was burning in the fireplace and happy red sparks died instantly at the classic fire screen. Heather had made some tuna-and-egg sandwiches and opened a bottle of red wine. They sat down by the fire, munched on their sandwiches and sipped the red wine.

After a while, Heather said, "You know, there was a time when Greta and I were good friends, but it all changed the day I caught her fondling one of the sales girls. I was so stunned, I just turned and went upstairs. For hours, I thought about what to do and finally decided to speak to Greta and leave it at that. Mind you, it wasn't easy, but I needed Greta. I told her that her behavior was unacceptable and that it mustn't happen again in the store. She just glared defiantly at me with those ice blue eyes and walked out.

"We never touched on the subject again. I figured it was none of my business and what she did in private was her affair. Our relationship remained cordial, but something between us had changed, and we both knew it. And then you showed up."

Elodie looked at her questioningly, and Heather continued, "The day I hired you, Greta stormed into my office after you had left and demanded to know what I intended to do with you. She had seen that arrangement you made and was resentful of your talent from the start. I'll never forget her expression when I told her that I had just hired you and hoped you would stay for a while—she looked like thunder, and her mouth was twisted into an ugly cavity. She left without saying a word. Just slammed the door and was gone for a few days. The rest you know."

"She must have been a very tormented person," Elodie replied, frowning.

"I agree. But enough of the past. Let's look toward the future."

"Just one more question," Elodie said. "Do you think she killed herself, or was she murdered as the police allege?"

"My guess is that she took the poison and then drowned herself. She had nothing to look forward to: no job, no family of her own, no hobbies. There was no pleasure or joy in her life. She seemed to walk on the dark side without ever trying," Heather replied pensively.

It was getting late, and Elodie got up, took the wine glasses to the kitchen, thanked Heather for the evening and walked home.

The next morning, the world outside her window was covered by a white, glittering blanket. It had snowed overnight, and all looked peaceful and quiet. As it was Elodie's day off, she stayed in bed a little longer and read, finally crawling out of the warm linens to don a long, heavy bathrobe and make herself a cup of coffee. After a quick shower, she spent the next few hours rummaging through her apartment. As the snow had again started to fall, it was not a very inviting day to go for a walk. *Maybe tomorrow, if the sun is shining*, she thought to herself.

But the sun did not shine, and the snow kept on falling. The ploughs had a hard time keeping the roads open for traffic, and the residential streets stayed un-ploughed. Elodie did not mind. She put on her black fur-lined boots and walked to the shop. The moment she entered, she felt that something was wrong. It was not yet time to open, but there were already people there. She was squeezing along the wall to get to her workstation when Heather called to her.

"Elodie, I'd like to introduce you to some of Greta's family. They've come from Door County to invite us to her funeral tomorrow."

Elodie greeted the strangers. She found it strange that they had come here when they could as easily have phoned. But seeing Heather's panic-stricken expression, she merely said, "Of course we'll come. When do you want to leave?"

"Within the hour," one of the younger men replied. "The weather is ghastly, and it will take us longer than usual."

"That works for me," she replied. "I'll get my car, and Heather and I can follow you."

She turned around and left the way she had come in, and within thirty minutes, she was back at the store. They put Heather's travel bag on the back seat, and the convoy left.

"Thank you for coming with me," Heather whispered, distraught. "I don't know what this is all about, but it doesn't feel quite right. Please stay by my side while we're there," she begged Elodie.

"Of course, don't worry. We'll find out what they want and why they came all this way instead of just calling you. Maybe they wanted to make sure that you were coming?"

"I just hope this doesn't have anything to do with that old family tradition that Frederik had told me about. You see, it was expected in their families that one of the daughters would look after the aging parents. Now that Greta is gone, perhaps there is no daughter left to look after her mother, and they want me to fill that role."

"But they can't sincerely think that you'd take that on? You have no connection with them, and on top of that, you have a business to run."

"Their family traditions are more important to them than anything else."

They continued the journey in silence, each deep in her own thoughts. After a few hours, they passed Green Bay and continued north along the shoreline for some time before the road turned inland. When they reached Sturgeon Bay, Elodie knew they were on the final leg of their journey and breathed a sigh of relief—it was only seventeen more miles to Egg Harbor. The day was waning, and they were glad when they saw the glittering lights of the small village spreading along the Niagara Escarpment on the waters of Green Bay.

They followed Greta's relatives to the outskirts of the village and arrived at a small farm, where a warm light spread its inviting glow on the porch. Heather and Elodie walked through the open door and found

70

themselves in a spacious kitchen filled with people. Greta's brother welcomed them and introduced both women to the people in the room. They were mostly smiling, and Elodie was struck by how much they resembled one another, with their blond hair and blue eyes. Even Heather fit right in.

Someone urged them to eat, and Elodie saw that the table and sideboard were laden with bowls of fresh fruit, little homemade hors d'oeuvres with smoked salmon and herrings, pickled vegetables in pretty porcelain bowls, a variety of nuts and dried berries, freshly baked breads, sweet and salted butter and an assortment of cheeses. As she was helping herself to the savories, she bumped into a tall, handsome man. She turned to apologize, and the man handed her a glass of white wine.

"From our very own winery," he said. "I hope you enjoy it."

Elodie took a sip and had to admit that the wine was very good, not too sweet yet with a hint of fruity flavors. She looked at the tall stranger who had handed her the glass and found herself gazing into eyes that were a startling blue, as blue as a summer sky. His freshly washed hair was the same color as Greta's, an unusual pale blonde, and an irresistibly devastating grin spread over his face, giving him a boyish look.

"I'm Mike," he said, bending slightly toward Elodie. "Greta was my aunt."

"Elodie Thorn," she replied. "I work for Heather Brown at the flower store."

"Ah, Heather—is she here? I must talk to her before

she leaves. I remember visiting her and Frederik with Aunt Greta when I was a small boy." He went in search of Heather, leaving Elodie alone with her glass of wine in her hands. She was studying the guests when an older woman dressed in black wobbled toward her.

"I am Greta's mother, Ida," she said matter of factly. "I have prepared a room for you and Heather for tonight. It is getting cold, and you will be warm and comfortable here."

Before Elodie could reply, the woman walked away.

Just then, a clergyman entered and the crowd fell silent. He announced that the funeral service would be held the next morning at ten o'clock in the little chapel overlooking the cold waters of Green Bay. Everybody nodded, and the conversations resumed while the clergyman mingled and helped himself to food and wine.

Heather came over to Elodie and whispered in her ear, "They've made up a room for us here in the house, and, even though I don't fancy staying here, I think we should. Do you mind sharing a room with me?"

"Of course not," Elodie replied. "Greta's mother just told me. I would like to go to sleep soon, though. The drive here was grueling, and I need to rest. I assume we're driving back tomorrow after the service?"

"Yes," Heather replied, and she went in search of a cousin who could show them to their room.

Their second-floor bedroom was warm and cozy. Elodie slipped between the sheets and was asleep in no time. The next morning, they descended the narrow staircase to the kitchen for breakfast, then made the short walk to the chapel where the service was to be held. Despite her unpleasant memories of Greta, Elodie was moved by the stories of Greta's life that family and friends told. Afterwards, as the congregation left, Heather and Elodie briskly marched back to the house, retrieved their travel bags, said good-bye to Greta's mother and a couple of cousins and started on their way back.

As they drove, talking about the funeral and Greta's family, the conversation led back to the worries Heather had expressed on the way there.

"Did you find out who will be caring for Greta's mother?" Elodie asked, concentrating on the wet road.

"I did," Heather replied. "When I spoke to one of the cousins, she reminded me that Ida has another daughter who can care for her. You cannot imagine the relief I feel! I have to admit that it was silly of me to jump to conclusions, but when I saw these men that I hadn't seen in so many years, I got frightened, and the old stories Frederik had told came back to me."

"But why did they come to the store instead of calling you?"

"They had some business in Chicago and thought it would be a nice gesture to pass by and invite me to the funeral."

That problem is solved, at least, until the next one appears, Elodie thought to herself. Little did she know how true her prediction would prove to be.

Toward evening, they arrived at the flower store, where Elodie dropped Heather off.

"Thanks for coming with me, Elodie," Heather smiled

tiredly. "Take the day off tomorrow. You've earned it."

"Thanks, Heather. Have a good night," Elodie answered, and she slowly drove toward her apartment.

11

A Special Occasion

THANKSGIVING WAS ONLY a week away, and Elodie was busy buying the ingredients for Thanksgiving dinner. She had invited Heather, together with a couple of coworkers without family, to join her for a home-cooked turkey dinner with all the trimmings. Each one of them was bringing a dish, leaving Elodie to cook the turkey with gravy, green beans and mashed potatoes. She was at the supermarket checkout, about to pay for her purchases, when she heard a familiar voice.

"Hi, Elodie."

She turned around and recognized the friendly face of the police officer who had brought the cell phone back to the store.

"Hi," she replied unenthusiastically.

"I see you're buying a turkey. Going to make a home-cooked meal?"

"Yes," she replied, "I've invited some women from the store to join me."

"That's good. It's not very pleasant to spend the holidays alone."

Elodie hurriedly finished her transaction and was attempting to make her escape when she felt him tugging on her sleeve. Annoyed, she turned around with a few short words on the tip of her tongue, but seeing his innocent face, she did not have the heart to let them escape her lips.

"Do you have time for a quick coffee at the coffee bar across the street?"

Against her will, Elodie smiled and accepted. He helped her put the groceries into her car, and they walked briskly across the street. They found a table by the window, ordered two coffees and sat silently until the coffee was served.

"Are you working on any interesting cases presently?" Elodie asked.

"If you're thinking of murder and mystery, no. There are a few robberies we're investigating, and hopefully we'll be able to apprehend the perpetrators soon."

As they talked about this and that, a tall stranger came through the door and approached their table. Adam greeted him—it was obviously somebody he knew—and offered him a seat. Elodie was taken aback; she knew this man. It was Mike from Egg Harbor.

"What are you doing here?" she blurted out.

"Elodie, what a nice surprise to see you here," he said, smiling.

"You two have met before?" Adam interjected in

surprise.

"Yes," replied Mike, "at my aunt's funeral a few weeks ago."

Adam fell silent while Elodie and Mike continued a lively conversation. They laughed easily together, and Elodie felt as if she had always known him. After a while, Adam got up and left, but Mike and Elodie barely noticed as they continued their conversation. It turned out that Mike had accepted a job as detective in the neighboring town. He had found an apartment not far from the police station, in an old building constructed in the early 1920s. The exterior had been kept the way it had been originally, but the inside had been remodeled and brought up to the newest standards. The rent was not cheap, but Mike could afford it, and he was enjoying living alone for the first time in his life.

The waitress approached with the check, and Elodie realized with a shock that the coffee shop was about to close, and they were being invited to leave. They got up, smiling at each other, put on their coats and left arm in arm.

Night had descended on the world around them, and it was bitter cold. A sharp wind was blowing and Elodie involuntarily shuddered. Mike put his arm around her and pulled her closer to him. He softly took her face into his hands and kissed her—a slow, thoughtful and surprisingly gentle kiss. When he let go of her, Elodie was reeling, and she felt a warm glow flowing through her. No longer noticing the biting wind, she looked questioningly at Mike, who was gazing at her with his deep blue eyes. A sensuous light passed between them, and wordlessly Mike took her arm, walked her to his car, and opened the door for her. Without a moment's hesitation, Elodie climbed in and they drove off.

After a short drive, they arrived at his building and entered his apartment. Elodie was amazed at the elegant space that greeted her. Large area rugs were scattered over the dark hardwood floor. A large, comfortable sofa faced a wood-burning fireplace, with matching double chairs on either side. Small tables were placed all around, and colorful pillows were heaped on the floor. Modern lamps illuminated the space with a warm light.

Suddenly, Elodie's eyes caught a movement in the corner of the room. Curious, she went closer, and when she saw what it was, she couldn't help laughing. A sleepy dog was peering at her from under a few blankets.

"And who are you?" she asked.

"My name is Baxter," a voice behind her said. She turned and saw Mike standing there, strikingly good looking in gray slacks and a white shirt, and felt the force of his potent magnetism.

To defuse the situation, Elodie pointed at Baxter. "How old is he?" she asked.

"He's eight years old—an old gentleman. I've had him since he was a puppy, and when I accepted the job here, I figured I'd take him with me. He likes to sleep during the day, so it works out well. I drop by at lunchtime to take him for a short walk, and then he's good to go again until I come home after work."

As he talked, he slowly advanced toward Elodie, and

she felt a ripple of excitement. It frightened her. He swept her gently into his arms and kissed her with his eyes before tracing the soft fullness of her lips with his tongue. The touch of his lips on hers sent a shock wave through her entire body.

He released her, muttering, "Elodie, what have you done to me? I've never met a woman like you before."

Welcoming his confusion, she took a moment to catch her breath. She was fully aware of his masculinity and the magical pull it had on her. But she had to leave; she was not ready for a one-night episode. She gently extricated herself from his embrace. "My dear Mike," she whispered, "I have to go before we do something we might both regret in the morning. Please take me back to my car."

Mike shook his head ruefully but did as she asked. He waited until he was sure that her car would start, then drove away. Elodie arrived at her place a few minutes later and climbed the stairs, her arms full of groceries and her heart heavy. She dumped her purchases on the kitchen table and put the perishable things into the fridge. Her appetite gone, she skipped dinner, absentmindedly went to her bedroom and slipped between the cold sheets. Sleep was long in coming, and her unhappy thoughts chased one another.

Why didn't I stay? she chided herself. *I'd be in his arms and happy now. But would I be happy? What if it had been just a repeat of Silvanus?* She was not sure if moments of happiness would be enough to get her through the heartache that would invariably follow.

Tears welled up in her eyes, but as always, she suppressed them. She felt a tingling in the pit of her stomach when she imagined being crushed within Mike's embrace. She ached for his touch, and involuntarily her fingers started to caress her body—slowly at first, but then faster and faster. Her pulse beat in her throat as a wave of delight and relief washed over her. Elodie lay wide awake in her bed, wondering what had just happened. She had never felt anything like this. The feeling was of indescribable beauty, and she wished it would continue for a while longer. Warmth spread from her center of pleasure throughout her whole body, touching every part of her. For the first time since she had left California, she felt at peace with herself and her surroundings. Finally, she fell into a dreamless sleep.

A shrill sound woke her, and Elodie scrambled for her phone. It was Heather, concerned because it was already ten o'clock and Elodie had not shown up for work.

"I'm so sorry," Elodie said. "I overslept. I'll be there as soon as I can."

She took a quick shower, dressed and ran out of the house. Heather was waiting for her at the shop and greeted her with a smile.

"Good morning," she said. "I have a few arrangements for you to create. They're being picked up by this evening. Otherwise, I wouldn't have called you."

Elodie nodded and went to her worktable to make the arrangements. Disconnected thoughts were jumbled in her head, making it difficult for her to stay focused on the flowers. The hours passed unbearably slowly, and she could hardly wait for her shift to be over so she could go home. The day ended at last, however, and she fled to her apartment.

Arriving at her door, she was surprised to find a box of chocolates, a card, and a single white rose. She opened the card, and her spirits lifted when she saw that it was a note from Mike, apologizing for last night and asking her for a date sometime after Thanksgiving. He had written his phone number below his signature. Elodie put the rose into a sleek crystal vase and set it on her bedside table together with the card. The chocolates she put on the coffee table.

She was tempted to call Mike immediately but restrained herself; she did not want to look too eager. *I'll call him after Thanksgiving,* she promised herself.

The next few days passed by in a flurry of activity. They were very busy at the store, and in the evenings Elodie was occupied with preparations for the Thanksgiving dinner. At last, it was Thanksgiving Day, and Heather, Jean and Esther arrived at her apartment. Each had brought a dish, and they sat down at the table to a regal feast. They ate, drank wine and chatted all afternoon.

After the meal, Elodie brought out the dessert she had made, along with strong black coffee and grappa. When Heather took her first bite, she closed her eyes in delight.

"What is this, Elodie?" she asked. "It's delicious!"

"Tiramisu," Elodie replied. "It's made with ladyfingers dipped in coffee, layered with a whipped mixture of eggs, sugar and mascarpone cheese. It's very popular in Italy."

"Well, you've outdone yourself! This is definitely the high point of the meal," Heather said, and the other women agreed. Elodie basked in their praise, gratified at the success of her holiday dinner.

Around seven in the evening, the women left, a bit tipsy but happy, each to return to her own home. Elodie slumped down in her favorite chair by the window. She was tired but pleased with the afternoon. She drank one more cup of coffee before clearing the table and cleaning up the kitchen. Satisfied, she went to bed and promptly fell asleep.

Next morning, Black Friday, Elodie avoided going out. She remembered her mother making her go with her to shop for Christmas gifts on Black Friday; she had insisted on getting to the stores when they first opened at the crack of dawn. It was horrible, people pushing and shoving to buy the prized items. Once, Elodie had gotten separated from her mother, and she had never forgotten the panic she had felt at being lost among all those strangers. Even today, Elodie still felt frightened when she found herself in a large crowd. She got out of bed and made herself some coffee and toast with jam and cheese. As she munched on her breakfast, her thoughts turned to Mike, and she decided to call him after lunch.

She waited until after one o'clock, then dialed his number. The answering service came on and she left a message.

Now what do I do? she asked herself. *What if he*

doesn't return my call? She realized with alarm that the thought made her wince. But before she could work herself into a state of agitation, her phone rang. It was Mike.

"Thanks for the box of chocolates and the rose," Elodie said breathlessly.

"You're welcome. I owed you an apology," he replied.

"Don't mention it."

"What are you doing tonight? Would you have dinner with me? We can go anywhere you like," he said.

Elodie hesitated for only a moment before saying, "Sounds good to me. Do you like Mexican food? I know a pretty good restaurant not too far from here. I'll make a reservation."

"I haven't had Mexican food in years, but I trust your taste," he said, teasing. "Pick you up at seven o'clock at your place."

"Okay," she replied, and they hung up. She did not mind that their conversation had been brief. Whatever else they wanted to say, they could say face to face tonight.

With trembling fingers, she dialed the restaurant and made a reservation.

"Is this for a special occasion?" the receptionist asked.

"No, nothing special," Elodie answered, but she thought to herself, *Of course it's a special occasion, but you don't need to know that. This is my secret.*

12

Happy Days

PROMPTLY AT SEVEN o'clock, the doorbell rang, and Mike stood in the doorway holding a bunch of colorful flowers in his arms. He handed them to Elodie, saying, "I didn't know what kind of flowers you liked, so I chose several different colors and types."

"They're beautiful! Thank you so much."

She found a crystal vase in a high kitchen cupboard and arranged the flowers. It was a stunning bouquet and reminded her of flower fields she had seen in California. Returning to the living room, she put the flowers on the table, then grabbed her bag and coat, and they left.

The restaurant was a short drive away, and a corner booth had been reserved for them. The lighting was dim, and snatches of lively conversation floated by. Mike looked around and nodded in approval. Saltillo tiles covered the floor, and the walls were painted in hues of malachite and dark yellow. The colonial chairs with their high backs looked authentic, and white tablecloths covered the tables. Exposed wooden beams on the ceiling gave the interior a calming and charming look. Rustic wall sconces and chandeliers distributed a warm light. Soft mariachi music played in the background, transporting listeners to faraway Mexico.

"I like this place. And if the food is as good as it smells, then we'll have a fantastic meal," he said.

As soon as they were seated, warm, crunchy tortilla chips with spicy red and mild green salsas appeared in front of them. They both grabbed a chip, and Elodie dipped hers in the green sauce as Mike dipped his in the red. He popped it into his mouth and promptly gasped; the red salsa was fiery hot. Elodie had to smile; she knew what it felt like to have your palate burned by salsa. Mike gulped down his glass of water, and the waiter immediately refilled it and handed them menus.

There were so many choices that it took them a while to decide, but they finally settled on sharing an order of *queso fundido* as an appetizer, along with fish tacos for Elodie and *enchiladas Suizas* for Mike. It didn't take long for the appetizer to arrive, and they both ate with gusto. Elodie hadn't realized how hungry she was. She had eaten only a late breakfast and nothing since. Mike quietly munched on the *queso fundido*, an easy smile playing around the corners of his mouth.

"This is delicious," he remarked, looking sheepishly at Elodie. "I've never eaten this before. I can't wait for the main course."

He finished the plate, and a few minutes later, the main dish was served. They both savored their food, talking in between bites about this and that. When they had finished, the waiter collected their dishes and placed a dessert menu on the table.

"Any dessert?" Mike asked.

"I'd love to, but I'm full," Elodie replied.

"What about some coffee?"

"That would be great. I'll have mine black without sugar or milk."

Mike ordered two coffees. It was served hot and black, the way Elodie liked it. Smiling at Mike, she said, "If you'd like to savor something sweet, I have some leftover tiramisu. We could eat it at my place with more coffee. Only if you like, of course."

She blushed at her own courage and was relieved when Mike accepted. He paid the bill, and they walked back to the car. While they were in the restaurant, it had started to snow, and the streets were covered with a light dusting of white powder. Mike expertly maneuvered the car out of the parking lot and drove cautiously on the slippery street.

Soon, they arrived at her apartment. Elodie hung their jackets in the wardrobe by the front door and motioned Mike to follow her into the living room. He sat down on the dark-brown chintz sofa while Elodie busied herself in the kitchen, making coffee and putting the tiramisu into small white dessert bowls. When she came back, carrying a tray, she found Mike looking at the little picture she had bought years ago.

"Where did you find this painting?" he asked.

"I bought it at a street market in Cannes. I spent a weekend there while I was staying in Paris, learning French," she replied, putting the tray down on the coffee table.

Mike said, "You've been to Europe?"

"Just France. I didn't have the means to stay after the foreign-language course was over, although I would have loved to see more of the old world."

"I hope to one day visit there myself and see the sights. I already have a pretty good idea where I want to go and what I want to see," he replied with a dreamy expression in his eyes.

"In the meantime, let's have some dessert and drink the coffee before it gets cold," Elodie said, smiling.

They both sat down on the sofa, and when Mike tasted the dessert, he exclaimed, "This is fabulous! I love it. Will you make tiramisu for me on my birthday?"

"Of course! When is your birthday?"

"A week from today," he answered quickly.

"Is that so?" she asked, regarding him skeptically.

"Here's the proof." And he handed her his driver's license.

Elodie glanced at it and saw that his birthday was indeed next Friday and that he was only a couple of years older than she was. She gave the license back to him, saying, "Well, in that case, I shall make tiramisu for you. Do you want me to bring it over to your place, or do you want to come over here?" The moment the words left her mouth, she realized what she had said, and she blushed when she saw a flash of humor cross his face.

"I'd love to spend my birthday with you," he said simply, and took a sip of the strong black coffee.

Elodie was relieved, and they both finished their coffee and dessert while talking about their early lives. Mike told her what it had been like growing up in Door County, and they compared his experiences to Elodie's childhood in California. The two locales could not have been more different, and it seemed amazing that both places could be part of the same country.

"It's getting late. I'd better head home," Mike said at last, getting up. "Driving will be a challenge with all this snow."

He gently pulled Elodie up and gathered her into his arms. The touch of his lips on hers electrified her entire body, and she kissed him back with a hunger that surprised her. Raising his mouth from hers, he gazed into her eyes and whispered, "Elodie, you have bewitched me. All I want to do is to stay here and explore every inch of you."

In response, she drew his face to hers in renewed ardor, and her lips found their way instinctively to his. Gently, he disengaged himself from her embrace.

"I'll come by tomorrow afternoon and bring some dinner," he said. "Is that okay with you?"

Elodie nodded, and Mike left reluctantly, his hand lingering in hers for a moment. Standing in the middle of the room, her lips still moist and warm from his kiss, all her loneliness seemed to engulf her, leaving her with nothing but a devouring yearning. Slowly, she picked up the cups and bowls from the table and loaded them into the dishwasher, then went to lock the front door and turn off the lights.

She went into her bathroom and studied her reflection in the mirror. *What is it that attracts Mike to me?* she wondered. Her shiny, midnight-black hair fell softly on her shoulders and set off her charcoal gray, almond-shaped eyes. She had long black eyelashes, making her eyes the focal point of her face. Her lips were not as full as she would have liked, and there was a little mole under her left ear. A small upturned nose sat in the middle of her face, giving it a look of symmetry. She was of medium height and slightly plump— she had put on a few pounds since her college days. *I guess I could lose a bit of weight,* she thought. *Other than that, there isn't much I can do about my looks.*

With a sigh, she changed into her pajamas and went to bed, but sleep eluded her. Thoughts of Mike chased one another in her head. She could still feel his strong embrace and the sweet, velvet warmth of his kiss.

The next morning, Elodie busied herself by cleaning the apartment. It was difficult to keep her attention on the task at hand as her thoughts wandered from place to place. One moment, she was back with Silvanus at the nursery and her old life in California; the next, she was reliving her evening with Mike. Suddenly, uninvited, her thoughts turned to Hutch.

Where are you? Will I ever see you again? she silently asked herself, then resolutely tried to banish him from her mind. *I won't let your memory spoil my happiness with Mike.*

In the middle of her battle with her memories, the

doorbell rang. It was Mike, his arms full of food and a bottle of wine peeking out of his coat pocket.

"Let me help you," Elodie said, opening the door wide. She took some of the paper bags from him, and he followed her to the kitchen. As she was putting everything on the countertop, Mike came up behind her and wrapped his arms around her middle. The touch of his hands was almost unbearable in its tenderness, and she slowly turned around to face him. A spark of light shone in her eyes, and Mike tenderly kissed them, then the tip of her nose, and finally her soft mouth. Elodie trembled as Mike gently guided her to the bedroom and eased her down on the bed.

Slowly, ever so slowly, he started undressing her. First, he unbuttoned her checkered flannel shirt, then unhooked her lacy bra. His fingers softly traced the circle of her breast, and his lips caressed the hardened nipple, sending shivers through her. A muted moan escaped her throat as Mike continued his exploration of her body. He unzipped her jeans, pulled them down and dropped them on the floor. His strong hand slid across her silken belly and seared a path down her abdomen onto her thigh. His touch was soft and painfully teasing. Elodie sighed, utterly powerless to stop him.

He quickly undressed himself and lay down beside her. His hands moved gently down the length of her back and gathered her to his warm body. Instinctively, she curled up against him while his hands explored the soft lines of her waist. She felt the taut muscles on his back, and when he moved his body to partially cover hers, she moaned softly. His tongue explored the recesses of her mouth as he kissed her with tenderness and restraint. Her breasts tingled as they rubbed against his hairy chest, and her breath came in small gasps. She had never felt anything like this in all her life. Previously unknown passion raced through her, and his expert touch sent her to higher and higher levels of ecstasy while her body cried out for release. Her head was spinning, and when he finally entered her, their bodies undulated in rhythmic harmony. The dormant sexuality of her body had been awakened, and she exploded in a firework of a million stars as the hot wave of passion erupted through them both.

Spent, Elodie snuggled against Mike as sweet sleep overcame her. As her breathing became regular, Mike watched her in wonder. He had never desired a woman with such a fiery intensity, and his whole body was still shivering with the aftershock of their first sexual union. He softly traced the contours of her face, and a fleeting smile passed over Elodie's sleeping countenance. Smiling, he held her hot body tight to him until he fell asleep, too.

A couple of hours later, they awakened, hungry, but before Elodie could jump out of bed, Mike spoke in a raspy voice. "Here we are. We've both had our affairs, and you don't really know me; I certainly don't know you. I only know I don't want to let you go. So, where does that leave us?"

Elodie was startled at his tone and remained silent for a moment. Then she peered into his eyes—eyes that were like infinitely deep pools of blue water—and quietly said, "We'll figure it out. But now I'm hungry. Let's go and cook, and we can talk during dinner."

Without waiting for his reply, she went to take a shower. He joined her, and they splashed around for a while, then got out and dressed, feeling clean and refreshed.

As Elodie pulled the vegetables out of the fridge to start preparing their meal, Mike asked, "I need to let Baxter out. May I bring him over, or would you rather come to my place?"

"Bring him over while I wash the vegetables," she said.

After Mike left, Elodie went over the events of the afternoon in her mind and was amazed at her behavior. *I never knew that lovemaking was such an intensely pleasurable experience*, she admitted to herself as her body responded with a cry for more.

Mike was back within thirty minutes with Baxter in tow, as well as his pillow and water and food bowls. He put the pillow between the sofa and the chair, and Baxter, after greeting Elodie with his wet nose, made his way over to the pillow and promptly fell asleep.

Mike busied himself in the kitchen, and Elodie kept him company. He cooked pasta with shrimp and mussels drowned in a delicious cream sauce, and a mixed salad with homemade dressing on the side. While he cooked, Elodie set the table for two, folding the cloth napkins in neat triangles and setting candles out. She dimmed the light, and after he brought in his creation, he lit the candles and poured the bottle of red wine he had found in a specialty store.

"You should have become a chef instead of a

detective," Elodie jokingly said.

"Actually, I am a chef. I worked in a high-end restaurant in Milwaukee for three years as a chef but found that I didn't want to cook all my life. I was always interested in police work, so I changed careers."

Elodie had the feeling that there was more to this story than he was willing to divulge right then. Not wanting to press him, she put another forkful of pasta into her mouth, making it impossible for her to speak. Mike changed the subject and talked about his dog. When they had finished their meal, Elodie started to get up, but Mike gently pushed her back onto her seat.

"This is my treat. You just stay put, and I'll clear away the dishes," he said with a twinkle in his eyes. He disappeared and reappeared a few minutes later holding a tray laden with two cups of steaming coffee and two liquor glasses filled with a brown liqueur.

"I hope you like this," he said as he handed her one of the glasses.

Elodie took a sip and exclaimed, "This is wonderful! What is it?"

"It's amaretto," Mike replied. "It's a sweet, almond-flavored Italian liqueur, made from a base of apricot pits, almonds, or both."

He took her by the arm and gently guided her to the sofa, where they sat down and savored the liqueur. Elodie snuggled close to Mike and smiled up at him. "Thank you very much for the lovely dinner," she said. "It was delicious."

"Glad you liked it."

"What made you give up working as a chef? You're

obviously very talented."

"As I said, I just didn't feel like cooking on demand any more. It's a very hectic job, and when the restaurant I was working at changed owners, I figured it was as good a time as any to try my hand at police work. Mind you, I still enjoy cooking, but on my terms, when I want," he said testily.

Elodie looked at him warily and nodded. She instinctively sensed that this was a sore spot in his life, better left alone. They remained seated for a bit longer until Baxter came to investigate.

"Shall we go for a walk with him? Or do you want to stay here?" Mike asked, putting the leash on his dog.

"I'll come with you guys," answered Elodie, and took their coats from the closet. They bundled up and ventured into the cold winter evening. Baxter was happy to be outside and promptly attended to his business. The night was crystal clear and a myriad of shiny stars competed with the stern-looking full moon gazing down upon earth. The world felt peaceful under the white blanket of shimmering snow.

Elodie moved closer to Mike, and he put his arm around her shoulders. "You're cold, aren't you?" he said, looking down at her. "Let's go back to your place and get you warmed up."

They had just turned toward her apartment when a police siren broke the silence. Flashing lights came at them, and Mike stiffened.

"What is it?" Elodie asked with concern.

"I'm on standby. I just hope they won't call me. Not tonight; I have other plans," he said, looking at Elodie with a sparkle in his blue eyes. But alas, his cell phone rang, and when he answered, it was the call he had hoped to avoid.

"I have to go, Elodie. May I leave Baxter with you? I should be back within a couple of hours."

They arrived at her place, and Mike put Baxter on his pillow, kissed Elodie on her waiting lips and departed. His kiss had made her tingle all over, and she felt cheated. She went back to the sofa and tried to read but was unable to keep her thoughts focused on the story. Finally, she gave up and turned on the television. Hearing familiar voices, she felt less alone. Baxter was snoring on his pillow, and Elodie decided to go to bed herself. She realized suddenly that Mike didn't have a key, and she didn't dare leave the door unlocked.

"He'll just have to ring the doorbell, or if that doesn't work, call me. I'm sure he'll be able to figure it out," she said to herself as she ambled to her room. She slipped between the sheets and fell asleep without any difficulty.

Morning was breaking when, through a dreamy fog, she heard the doorbell ring. It took her only a few moments to realize that it must be Mike. She jumped out of bed, ran to the door in her pajamas, and quickly opened it to let him in. And there he was, tired looking but with a bag of fresh bagels in his arms.

"Good morning, Elodie," he said wearily as he handed her the bagels. "I need some strong, hot coffee. I thought I'd rather come here than sit all by myself at Starbucks."

Elodie pulled him into the apartment, took his coat

and sat him down on the sofa. "I'll make coffee; it'll only take a minute." She disappeared into the kitchen.

When she came back with two steaming cups of coffee, Mike was fast asleep on the sofa. She took his coffee back to the kitchen and covered him with a checkered throw, sat down in the chair and watched him sleep while she sipped her coffee.

She studied the lines of his face and wondered what they could tell her of his past. His long blond lashes softly rested on his tired countenance, and his alluring lips were slightly parted. Elodie felt an intense urge to kiss them. Just thinking about what his kisses had felt like made her quiver inside with an almost painful yearning.

As Elodie watched, Mike slowly opened his eyes and smiled at her, sending her heart racing.

"It was a long, cold night, and the warmth here just put me to sleep. I hope you'll forgive me," he said.

Instead of answering, she took his hand and guided him to her bedroom. She unbuttoned his shirt and pulled it off, then unzipped his pants and pulled them down as she gently pushed him onto the bed. All the while, Mike watched her intensely, his body responding violently to her caresses. He tried to grab her, but she escaped his grasp.

Laughing, she said to him, "Now it's my turn." She took off the rest of his garments and then undressed herself slowly under Mike's longing gaze. She shivered and joined him beneath the satin sheets. Her tickling fingers trailed up and down his abdomen and played with his nipples.

He moaned at her touch and whispered hoarsely, "Enough, Elodie. Please, I can't take it any longer."

Elodie looked at him tenderly, kissing his demanding lips and gently guiding him inside her. Their bodies melted against one another as the flames of passion exploded within them both. Spent, they lay side by side, breathing deeply.

After a while, Elodie saw that Mike was asleep. She got up, careful not to wake him, took a shower and dressed in comfortable wool pants and an old gray sweatshirt. She put on her coat and took Baxter out for a short stroll. Heavy clouds were gathering in the west; the weather station had forecast more snow for this afternoon. She pulled the coat closer to her body and dragged Baxter away from a piece of bone he was investigating. Back at her apartment, Baxter went to sleep, and Elodie checked her email.

A few hours had passed when a still sleepy Mike appeared in the doorway. "I have to go home and shower, then drop by the office," he said. "May I come back afterwards if you can stand another evening in my company?"

Elodie, smiling at his earnest expression, got up from her desk and walked toward him. He bent down and gently brushed her mouth with his lips. "I take that as a yes?"

"We can have dinner here. They've announced a snow storm brewing in the west, so we'd better stay in."

He nodded and went to take Baxter, but Elodie said, "Leave him here. He's nicely asleep. I took him outside earlier."

"Thanks, Elodie," Mike said, and left the apartment.

13

The Holidays

THE NEXT FEW months flew by, and suddenly, Christmas was just around the corner. The weather played its part, and the village was covered by snow glistening in the moonlight. The days were short, and a bitter cold wind blew from the north, but Elodie did not mind. Her world was sunny and warm. Mike came over almost every night. Sometimes they would go out for a bite to eat, but most evenings they stayed in.

Elodie was busy at the shop, creating the most beautiful arrangements reflecting the white season. Heather was delighted with the way Elodie's creations helped increase her shop's profits, so when Elodie asked her for a couple of days off after Christmas, Heather readily agreed.

"I thought of closing the store for a few days starting on December twenty-four around four o'clock and reopening for regular hours on December twenty-seventh. We can do the same for the end of the year, closing at four on December thirty-first and reopening January third. What do you think?"

"I like that. That gives everybody the chance to spend the holidays with their families. Thank you, Heather."

Over the weekend, Elodie and Mike went to the Christmas tree lot and chose a small tree, which they proudly took home to Elodie's place. They spent the entire afternoon decorating it, and when they were done, Mike stepped back to admire the result. Dark red bows gave the tree an air of gladness; some old glass ornaments, found at an estate sale, shimmered in the dim light; and small bells and frosted fruit hung from the branches, with colorful birds resting on them. Pine cones and dried flowers peeked out from among the twigs, and rows and rows of small, teardrop-shaped lights glowed softly, illuminating the sparkling Christmas star sitting on top like a beacon of peace, giving the tree a serene look.

"This is really quite exquisite. I've never seen a Christmas tree like this. You're very talented."

"Thanks" Elodie said modestly.

"Do you want to go out for dinner or shall we cook something here?" he asked.

"I'd rather stay home. Do we have something in the fridge?"

"I've made some pumpkin ravioli the other night and brought a batch over. We can have them with some butter."

"Sounds divine, let's go cook. I'm hungry."

So, both went to the kitchen and Elodie watched him prepare their dinner. They sat down on the sofa with their plates and enjoyed the food and each other's company. They discussed their plans for Christmas and agreed to have dinner at home on Christmas Eve. Then, on Christmas Day, they would drive to a nearby town, well-known for its Christmas decorations, and have a late lunch there, provided the weather stayed calm.

The weather gods were benevolent, and the days were filled with sunshine. It was bitter cold, but the countryside looked very festive in its white glittering cape. This was the most cheerful Christmas Elodie had ever had, and she wished it could last a little longer. On New Year's Eve, Mike was called away but made it back just in time to clink a glass of champagne with Elodie and to wish her a happy new year.

Elodie had quickly learned that it was useless to ask him where he had gone. The first time she had asked, he had answered curtly, "I can't tell you as this is an ongoing investigation. So please, don't ask, okay?"

"Okay," she replied, and did not ask again.

They watched a movie and then went to sleep. Next morning, when Elodie awoke, Mike had left. Panic overcame her, but before she could get her bearings, a wet nose greeted her. It was Baxter. She laughed out loud just as Mike came through the door with a tray of steaming coffee, buttered toast, jam and Brie.

"What's so funny?" he asked.

"Baxter woke me and tickled me with his wet nose," she replied.

He put the tray on the little bedside table, and they drank the black coffee and munched on the toast.

"You are a treasure; how do you know so well how to treat a woman?"

"It's a long story," he replied, a shadow hastening over his eyes as he started to tell the tale.

He had been in his teens when he met Adele. She was about ten years older and was experienced in what women like. Mike had fallen head over heels for her, and she had taken him under her wing. She had taught him how to arouse a woman. How to make her yearn for his touch by slowly exploring her body, and how to reach fulfilling release from lovemaking. How to kiss in different ways, lovingly, hungrily, demandingly. That summer had been the best time he had ever had. He had thought that it would never end, but it had. One day, Adele had left without even a good-bye. Mike had been heartbroken and had tried for weeks to find out where she had gone. Her family had pretended not to know, and after some time, Mike had given up.

He had gone to Milwaukee to become a chef because Adele adored excellent food—somehow, cooking those delicious meals had made him feel close to her. However, soon he'd had to admit that he didn't want to be a chef for the rest of his life, and he had changed careers. He had become a detective, and when he had been offered a job in the neighboring village, he had taken the opportunity and moved.

Elodie watched him closely as he talked and had the sinking feeling that this Adele was still very much in his system. *I just hope that she will never surface again,* she thought.

"Now you know," he said flatly, and took a sip of coffee.

"Shall we go to the mall and find a new dog bed for Baxter and some bones to chew on?" she said lightly.

Mike looked at her and nodded. "Thanks for not pestering me with more questions," he said, kissing her lightly on her soft lips. "Let's get ready and go." He got out of bed and into the shower while Elodie observed him silently.

At the mall, they found a cute dog bed and Nylabones for Baxter. With their purchases under their arms, they returned to the car and hurried home to watch Baxter inspect his new bed and chew on his new bones. He was rolling happily on his soft bed making funny dog faces, interrupted by low yaps, so that both Elodie and Mike had to laugh out loud. By the time Baxter fell asleep, Mike's dark mood had dissipated, and Elodie wondered if she had imagined his lingering attachment to Adele.

14

A Meeting in Door County

NOW THAT THE new year had come, life went on as before. They both went to work during the day, spending most evenings together, and soon it was springtime. Elodie loved the spring with its sweet fragrance, the soft green of budding leaves and the happy chirping of birds. As the days grew longer and warmer, Elodie's flower creations changed to match the season. She took pleasure in her job and was grateful that Mike was in her life.

If Mike was off on a weekend, they would go exploring the countryside. There were so many small villages to visit. One of Elodie's favorite places was Galena on the banks of the Mississippi, with its many little stores filled with souvenirs and knickknacks lining the main thoroughfare. Once, on Main Street, they had found a small store with a display of colorful crystals in many different sizes. Elodie had bought a small crystal with a mechanism to make it twirl. She hung it in her kitchen window, and when the sun's rays hit it just right, it made fairy lights dance on the wall.

Elodie loved these outings and believed that the past with its sad experiences had lost its grip on her. Only rarely did she wonder why Mike never suggested they move in together or made any comments about a future together. She did not press him, assuming that he needed time before he made any commitment to her. As spring turned into summer with its intense heat and humidity, instead of driving out into the countryside, they went to the beaches on Lake Michigan. Often, they packed a lunch and just lay in the sun, enjoying the day off.

One summer's eve, Mike told her that he would be going to Door County and would like to take her with him to meet his family. He did not elaborate further, so Elodie just looked at him and nodded. They planned to leave in two weeks and stay there over a long weekend.

When she asked Heather for the days off, the latter smiled and asked, "Is Mike finally getting serious?"

"He hasn't said anything other than he wants to visit his family in Egg Harbor and would like to take me along. I'll tell you more when we get back."

"Have a good trip, and give my regards to Frederik's family."

"I will." And Elodie left, in high spirits.

The drive to Door Country was uneventful, and Elodie watched the lush, green landscape pass by. Her eyes followed a pair of falcons soaring high in the blue summer sky, and she wondered what it would be like to be able to soar higher and higher, well above the clouds where the sun always shone.

Mike's voice brought her back and she looked at him.

"Dreaming, Elodie?" he asked.

"I guess just wondering what life would be like above the clouds."

Mike laughed, and Elodie asked him what the special celebration was all about.

"July twenty-ninth is the feast day of Norway's first Christian king, Saint Olav, who was killed in battle in 1030 when he tried to Christianize Norway. His body was taken to Trondheim and buried by the Nidelven River. People experienced miracles at his grave, and he came to be worshipped as a saint. You know, during Saint Olav Festival, pilgrims from all over Europe come to the services at Nidaros Cathedral. In the middle ages, it was customary to stay awake before an important, solemn festival, and to this day, the main celebration takes place on July twenty-eighth and continues through the following night. It is a time for meditation in the heritage of Olav," he explained.

"Have you ever been to his grave site?"

"No, but some of my relatives have. You'll meet them tonight when the festivities begin."

The time flew by as they talked, and soon they entered the village of Egg Harbor. As they drove up to his parents' house and parked, Mike's mother came out to greet them. She bore an unmistakable resemblance to her sister Greta, and Elodie felt right at home with her.

"Come in, come in," she said. "You must be tired after your long drive. I have prepared your rooms. Mike, you'll stay in your old room, and Elodie can have the guest room. I hope this will be comfortable for you?" she said, turning to Elodie.

"Of course," Elodie answered, and followed her inside.

Mike took their bags and showed her to her room. He set the bag on the chair and pulled Elodie close to him.

"My mother is a bit old fashioned—unless you're married, you don't sleep in the same room." He smiled and brushed her waiting mouth with his soft lips. She tried to hold him, but he pulled away, laughing.

"Not now, Mother is watching."

Elodie looked around the room, liking what she saw. There was a queen-sized, old-fashioned bed with a dark wooden headboard and matching nightstands on each side. A colorful bedspread covered the linens, and Elodie wondered whether it came from the old country. She had certainly never seen anything like it. The heavy curtains made of dark-green fabric were already drawn, and a soft light shone from a lamp standing in the corner.

She freshened up, and as she opened the door, she heard Mike's mother say to someone standing in the shadows, "She is here. I thought she was gone for good, but now she is back, stirring up all these painful memories again."

Mike came out of his room, and together they went

downstairs to the kitchen, which was filled with relatives and friends. On the table and sideboards, platters and bowls were piled with traditional Norwegian food. In addition to pickled herring, there were poached fish, grilled fish, smoked fish, salted fish, dried fish and cured fish, as well as fish soup and a variety of smoked salmon. There were also cold cuts and vegetables with different dips and a variety of crackers, potato chips, and hard and soft cheeses. In one corner, a temporary bar had even been installed, where all types of drinks were available: beer, wine, water, fruit juices and sodas.

Mike introduced Elodie to all the people, and she felt right at home among them. She was very happy to be part of this great extended family. Pieces of conversation floated around, laughter erupted and everybody was having a good time. Suddenly, the room went quiet, and all heads turned toward the entrance. A middle-aged blond woman, her full red lips parted slightly, stood in the door frame. Elodie was mesmerized by her.

Somebody close to her whispered, "It's Adele."

The smile froze on Elodie's face, and she pressed her thin lips together hard. Involuntarily, her hand shot up to her face and covered her mouth to prevent a cry from escaping her throat. Her eyes sought Mike's, but he had eyes only for Adele. She had never seen such a look of rapture on his face before. He slowly made his way toward the woman and kissed her on both cheeks. Adele looked at him, and Elodie knew right then that she was losing Mike. Adele had such magnetism that even

Elodie was drawn toward her. She started to speak, and her voice was like a silver melody carried by angels' wings, soft and deep. The men looked at her in fascination while the women gazed apprehensively at their husbands and sons.

Elodie stayed back and watched the scene unfolding before her eyes. It was obvious that everybody in this room—probably in the whole village—knew about the long-ago affair between Adele and Mike. She caught the eyes of some of the other women, who were looking at her with compassion.

Mike's mother made her way toward Elodie and pulled her into an empty room. "We had no idea that Adele would dare show up here," she said, gazing sympathetically at Elodie. "Did Mike tell you about her?"

"He mentioned her before we came up here, but I assumed that it was just a teenage episode and long forgotten."

"I hate to say this, but Adele has some hold on Mike—always had and I fear always will."

Elodie just looked mutely at her. What could she say? What could she do? She decided to act unconcerned so as not to worry Mike's mother. They went back to the kitchen and mingled as if nothing had happened. Elodie caught sight of Mike just as he was leaving with Adele through a side door. She finished her lukewarm drink, said good night to her hostess and quietly climbed the stairs to her room. Slipping between the sheets, she prayed that sleep would come quickly. For once, her prayer was answered, and sleep overcame her, giving welcome relief from her troubled thoughts.

When Elodie woke up, the sun stood high in the sky. She quickly showered, dressed and went downstairs. Mike was sitting at the kitchen table, sipping a cup of coffee and staring at the wall. When he heard her come in, he looked up, his eyes filled with turmoil, and motioned her to sit beside him.

"I would like to head back now, if that's okay with you," he said stiffly.

Elodie nodded and said, "I'll get my bag. I've already packed."

They said their good-byes to his family and left. The drive back was joyless and seemed endless as a heavy silence stood between them. Mike just concentrated on the road without addressing her, not even once. He dropped her off at her apartment and mumbled something about work. Elodie disappeared wordlessly into the building.

With a heavy heart, she climbed the stairs and unlocked her door. The apartment felt cold, as if all the happiness had been sucked out while she was gone. She carried the bag into her bedroom and slumped down on the sofa. Thoughts chased one another incessantly as she tried to recall the events of the past few days.

Everything had seemed fine between her and Mike the day they left for Door County. She had felt sure that Mike loved her. They had spent almost every night together since Christmas, and she had hoped that he would soon propose to her. The only time she recalled having felt a chill run down her back was on the morning he had told her about Adele, when for a few moments, he had become very distant. But then he had been quickly his old self again, and she hadn't given it any further thought. She'd had no idea how deep-rooted his love for Adele was and that it would eventually destroy hers.

15

Alone

AS SUMMER PASSED and gave way to autumn, Heather was watching Elodie closely. She knew that something had changed since her trip to Egg Harbor. Elodie's work was as beautiful as ever and skillfully incorporated branches of fruit trees and stalks of corn and wheat to reflect the harvest season, but the arrangements spoke loud and clear of her inner turmoil. She did not intrude upon her; she hoped that one day Elodie would confide in her.

One day, toward the end of September, Elodie asked for a couple of days off, and Heather jokingly said, "You're not going to elope, are you?"

Elodie shook her head, and Heather could read all the pain and suffering in her gray eyes. She put her arm around Elodie's shoulder and said, "Take a week off and rest. When you come back, you will feel better."

She gently pushed her out the door and watched her shuffle to her car. Her heart ached for the girl, but she knew she could not address these issues yet. She had to wait until Elodie invited her.

ᘓ

ELODIE SLOWLY drove home to her empty apartment. Mike had come over only once since their trip up north and had not stayed the night. Elodie had known that it was over, but she had needed Mike to tell her so. Until that evening, she had held on to her hopes, but now they were crushed, never to be resurrected. Her thoughts turned to that fateful evening, and suddenly she was reliving the pain all over again.

ᘓ

SHE TURNED INTO her street, and saw Mike's car parked along the sidewalk in front of her building. Tiny sparkles of hope bubbled up in her heart, and she quickly parked her car and almost ran upstairs. Mike was waiting for her, and with trembling fingers she unlocked the door.

"Can I offer you something?" she asked, but Mike shook his head.

He took her hands into his, gazed into her eyes and said, "I came to say good-bye. I'm leaving town and won't be returning."

"Adele?"

He just looked at her without answering her

question.

"Please don't go," Elodie whispered, but Mike let go of her hands, turned away and made for the door. He opened it, walked through it, closed it. Elodie was left standing in the middle of the room, feeling icy fingers seep into her every pore. The bright world outside, together with her future, suddenly turned dark, an ominous dark, and with a deep, unaccustomed pain in her breast, she slowly sunk down to the floor and hugged her knees, rocking slowly back and forth.

"He just walked out of my life, the way he walked in only a few months ago," she muttered as a suffocating sensation tightened her throat. She wanted to cry, but no tears flowed. She wanted to scream in agony, but no sound left her mouth. She wanted to pound the floor, but her fists stayed clenched in her lap. All she could do was endure and wait until her mind regained power over her body. She closed her eyes, her heart aching with intense pain.

After what seemed to her hours, she got up and walked mechanically into the kitchen. She sat down at the kitchen table, her head between her hands, and tried to make sense out of what had just happened. She was unable to think straight, and only two thoughts kept coming back: *Mike is gone,* and *I am alone again.*

When darkness enveloped her, she walked to the den and lit a candle. The small flame spread a warm little glow on the coffee table, but it was not enough to reach her heart. She felt the cold gripping her, numbing it, as she sat in lonely silence. When night fell, she sluggishly got to her feet and dragged herself to her bedroom. It was cold as she slipped between the sheets and pulled the blanket up to her face. With unseeing eyes, she stared into the unyielding dark until sleep finally had mercy on her and released her from the day's pain.

♋

ELODIE ARRIVED AT her apartment, glad to have a few days off. Next morning, she got up, made herself a cup of coffee and forced herself to eat a piece of toast with cheese and jam. Initially, she had intended to drive down to Tennessee and visit Nashville, but now, she had lost interest in sightseeing. She found a book that she had wanted to read for a long time, but she could not keep her mind on the story. Her thoughts were preoccupied with Mike and the end of their relationship. It was painful to think that he would never hold her again, kiss her or make love to her. She could still feel his strong arms around her. With a sigh, she got up and wandered aimlessly around the apartment.

The day was stormy, mirroring her own emotions, and suddenly she decided to go to the city. She walked to the station and took the next train to Chicago, and within the hour, she had arrived at the main terminal and exited the busy station toward the lake. She passed Millennium Park and strolled beside the water. The waves were pounding the shore, and only a few people had ventured outside. A storm was brewing, and Elodie headed back to the Art Institute of Chicago to look at some of the paintings she so liked. When she reached the painting *A Marine*, by George Inness, she stood before it and studied the roiling sea, the sky dark with clouds, illuminated only by patches of white and orange light that outlined the ships and the distant town on the horizon, and two lonely seagulls flying toward the light.

If only I could follow the seagulls to find the light in the darkness surrounding my soul, she thought as she made her way to the next painting. It was *After a Summer Shower,* by the same painter. The darkness of a rain shower had given way to a faraway rainbow, and the white clouds reflected the sunshine. A narrow path, bordered on one side by green, leafy trees, led to a distant village.

Follow the narrow path, and if I stay the course, it will eventually lead me back to the light. Elodie stood a while longer by the painting and marveled at the artist who had so perfectly portrayed her feelings and given her the means to find her way out of the darkness that enveloped her. She spent another couple of hours wandering through the exhibition halls until it was time to walk back to the train station and go home.

The platform was crowded with commuters. However, Elodie found a seat by the window and looked out at the world passing by. The days had grown shorter, and she could see lights turned on in living rooms and kitchens. Arriving at her destination, she left the train and briskly walked home. When she entered her dark apartment, she felt the chilly shadow approaching, but she turned on lamps, lit the candles and started a fire in the fireplace. A warm glow permeated the rooms, and Elodie felt the shadow recede.

"I will find my way out of this darkness," she said, "the way George Inness's paintings have shown me."

Tired, but feeling much better than when she had left, she went to the kitchen, rummaged in her fridge and found some leftover spaghetti. She heated the food and ate it in the company of her television. She watched for a couple of hours, flipping from one channel to another, then went to bed.

She spent the next few days cleaning out her apartment, taking clothes and other possessions she no longer used to the thrift store, then stopped at the mall and bought herself a new outfit, together with a new pair of shoes.

On Monday morning, when her alarm clock pierced the silence, Elodie woke up feeling more optimistic than she had in a long time. Arriving at the shop, she cheerfully greeted her coworkers and began creating the flower arrangements needed for the day. She put several pots in different sizes and colors on her work-table and filled them with floral foam. A couple of glass vases, an empty bottle and an empty tea tin were also waiting there.

She lined the bottoms of the bigger glass vases with glittering white gravel. In the smaller glass vases, she put some greenery and filled them with white hydrangeas, white roses and lilies of the valley. She then inserted the smaller vases into the bigger ones and set them on the shelf. The empty bottle she filled with water and added stems of white yarrow and white lilies, some green leafy fillers and one blood-red rose. In the red tea tin, half filled with floral foam, she stuck white begonias, other small white flowers and a couple of green grasses. As she was putting them on the shelf with the others, Heather came over and looked astonished at her creations.

"What made you use these unusual containers? And why the white flowers?" she asked, intrigued.

"I just felt like doing something different. Don't you like them?"

"Yes, I like them very much, and I'm sure they'll sell in no time." She went to greet a customer and brought her over to the shelf where Elodie's creations were patiently waiting.

"Oh, these are exquisite," the elegant woman exclaimed, and she bought the arrangements in the glass vases.

"What did I tell you?" Heather said to Elodie. "People do like flowers arranged in unusual ways. You really have an eye for that. Want to come upstairs after work so we can chat for a while?"

"Sounds good," Elodie replied, not feeling in the least like visiting with Heather but having no good excuse. She continued creating flower arrangements, but her mind was far, far away. Again she went over the day when Mike had left her, and a searing pain squeezed her heart. She could not walk around with this heavy misery; she had to do something to relieve the agony inside her. So, in her mind, she took all the hurt, the memories and the happy moments with Mike and laid them in a small painted box, then hid it deep in her heart where no one would ever find it. *Hopefully, one day I will be able to open the box and look at the*

person next to her. It was the same with eating out. Occasionally, she forced herself to go to a sit-down restaurant and order some nice food for herself. But she had no one to share her thoughts with, and every time she was disappointed.

"I have to be careful not to become a quirky old spinster," she admonished herself. She had thought about signing up for one of those Internet dating sites; the single women at the shop each used a dating site, and they loved it. But so far, she had not found the courage to do so.

On Saturday morning, she went to the store—it was open for a few hours to give customers the opportunity to pick up their orders—and found Heather arranging some flowers. Heather was pleased to see Elodie and said, "Hi, Elodie, come to help me? I've been quite busy."

Just then, some more customers came through the door, and among them was the elegant lady who had purchased the glass vases. She spoke to Heather and pointed at Elodie.

"Come over here for a moment, please," called Heather, and Elodie went over to them.

"I really love your arrangements," the woman said. "Could you create some for me today? I know it's short notice, but we have unexpected guests and I need some table centerpieces."

Elodie glanced briefly at Heather, then nodded. "How many do you need?"

"Three would be wonderful. Two smaller ones and one big one, preferably in yellow, if possible," she said.

"They will be ready by two o'clock," Elodie said, and she walked to her workstation to get started.

Heather and the woman talked for a while longer, and after she had left, Heather came over to her. "I need to talk to you," she said. "Please join me for a glass of wine after work." She did not wait for an answer but walked to her office.

When the arrangements were made and the woman had picked them up, Elodie closed the store and, glad she did not have to spend the afternoon alone, went upstairs to find Heather. She was seated in one of the chairs facing the fireplace, where a cheery fire was spreading its warmth throughout the room.

"Come sit with me. I have poured you a glass of red wine."

When Elodie was seated, Heather looked at her and quietly said, "This morning, Mike's mother called to tell me that Mike has married Adele, and they have left the country together for an unknown destination. I thought you should know. I'm so sorry, Elodie. I can imagine how this must make you feel. If there is anything I can do, please let me know."

The color drained from Elodie's face, and she sat as still as a wooden statue. Her gray eyes were wide open, glazed over with a look of despair. Her hands clasped one another, and her fingernails dug deep into her flesh, but she did not feel the pain. A sensation of intense sickness and desolation swept over her as an inner torment began gnawing at her. Thoughts were spinning in her head, but she was unable to grasp a single one of them. All she knew was that Mike was gone from her life forever.

It took her a few minutes to compose herself, but then she whispered in a toneless voice, "Thank you for telling me. Now, I can go on with my life as hope of Mike ever returning just vanished." She took the glass and gulped down the sweet wine in one long swallow. When she looked up at Heather, her eyes were dry, and she seemed almost relieved.

"You're amazing," Heather said. "Any other woman would have been destroyed by this news, but you just go on as if nothing has happened. Did his love not touch you? Are you so cold, or do you have a secret for dealing with life that I don't know about?"

Elodie looked at her, pain lurking in her eyes. "I've learned to put painful memories away, never to look at them again until I feel that they've lost their hurt and become beautiful. I keep them tucked away in my heart forever. If I didn't, I wouldn't be able to go on. You understand?" she asked.

Heather nodded and hugged Elodie. "If you ever need anything, anything at all, please come to me," she said. "I'm sure together we can tackle anything the world throws our way."

"Thank you, Heather, I will."

They drank some more wine, each deep in thought, until Elodie got up and wished Heather a good evening. Snow had silently started to fall and covered the village with a clean white blanket of snow. She walked home briskly and soon arrived at her apartment. After lighting a fire in the fireplace, she sat down with a glass of red wine. As she stared at the dancing flames, she sent a prayer to heaven for Mike and Adele: *May you be happy together.*

CB

H EATHER W AS looking out at the white world, as well, still feeling surprised at Elodie's reaction to the news about Mike and Adele. *Every other person I know would have been upset or cried or blamed Adele for taking Mike away from her,* she thought. *But not Elodie; she just goes on as if nothing happened to turn her world upside down. She's one of only a few people I've met in my life who refused to be a victim. I wonder whether she'll ever confide in me.* Then she cleaned up the coffee table, put the wine glasses in the dishwasher and went to bed.

CB

N EXT MO RNING , Elodie was already at work before Heather came downstairs. She was selecting the containers she was going to use to make her arrangements. Heather watched her for a while before leaving her to her work. Just before lunch, she returned to see how the arrangements were coming along and gasped in amazement at what she saw. Elodie had filled simple white porcelain containers with floral foam and had created the most unusual designs yet. Each container held only flowers in the same color, with just one bent bloom in a contrasting hue, giving the arrangements a dramatic aspect.

"These are quite stunning," Heather said. "How do

come up with such a variety of arrangements?"

"I just follow my feelings," Elodie answered quietly, her eyes sad.

Heather said, "Let's go out for lunch at the little family diner at the corner of Main and Lake. My treat."

"Thanks."

They left the shop and walked the short distance to the diner. It had been in the same family for more than half a century, and neither the menu nor the warm and cozy interior had changed much during all that time. Heather and Elodie were shown to a booth by the window. To Elodie's surprise, the menu was quite extensive, and she ordered the liver with onions and apples. Heather ordered a burger with fries.

"You like liver?" Heather asked, astonished.

"Yes, I do, and whenever it's offered, I usually order it. I hardly ever cook it for myself."

"If you don't mind my asking you, how come you seem to go on as if nothing has happened to upend your world?"

"Ah, Heather, I saw firsthand how an event can crush you. My aunt—my mother's sister—was raped when she was young and never got over it. Whenever she met a man, she shied away because of what had happened to her. She avoided family gatherings and wallowed in self-pity. People were sympathetic at first, but after a while, they got fed up with having to cater to her feelings and started to ignore her. This, in turn, made her even more reluctant to have anything to do with anybody.

"I remember as a child that we were always told to

be quiet because Aunty was asleep upstairs or had had a bad day. I thought that it was such a waste of one's life to feel so sorry for oneself. Bad things happen to people, but that's not a good reason to give up living happily. I decided early on that I wouldn't become a victim of circumstances but find a way to cope with whatever life had in store for me.

"And there's one more thought that has always put things into perspective for me: you're never the only person in the world who has problems. There are thousands of people who've experienced the same cruel struggles."

"You're wise beyond your years," Heather responded.

"I don't know about that; I only know that I'm the one responsible for my happiness. I can't hand it over to someone else."

"Thank you for being so honest with me. I appreciate it."

The food arrived and they ate in silence, then drank their black coffees. Heather paid the bill, and the two unlikely friends left the restaurant to return to their work.

ᘓ

CHRISTMAS WAS just around the corner, and Elodie was busy creating flower arrangements for the season. She used a variety of Christmas decorations in her creations, and they looked stunning. Increasingly, customers were requesting that she make special arrangements for their tables and fireplace mantels, as well as some to be given as gifts. Elodie enjoyed creating unique pieces, always trying to imagine what the customer was like, and the appearance of the rooms where her arrangements would be placed.

One day, a woman who had been a regular customer for a while asked Heather if Elodie would be able to come to her house and see where the flowers would be displayed. Heather called to Elodie and introduced her to the woman. "This is Mrs. Nelson. She lives in the neighboring village and would like you to go to her house to see the display areas for your arrangements."

Elodie greeted Mrs. Nelson with a smile and said, "Of course I can. When is it convenient for you?"

"Maybe tomorrow around noon? Why don't you both come, and I'll have some lunch brought in. What do you think, Heather?"

"We'll be there tomorrow around noon," Heather said.

"See you for lunch." And Mrs. Nelson walked out of the store.

"What was that all about?" Elodie asked Heather. "Why does she want us to go there?"

"Ah, Elodie, small village inhabitants, especially the ones with money, are always in competition with one another. I suppose she's having a Christmas party and wants to make sure that she has the most spectacular centerpiece of all her neighbors."

"Well, if that will make her happy, I shall pay attention and create something special for her."

They smiled at one another, and each went back to her work.

Next day, promptly at noon, Heather and Elodie rang Mrs. Nelson's doorbell. The door was opened by her housekeeper, who showed them into the family room off the entrance. Walking through the huge, dark double door, Elodie was taken aback by the elegance of the home. A beautifully curved wooden staircase led to the upper floor. The railing was polished to a shine, and the chandelier was free of any dust. The family room was stunning, with tall windows framed by nutmeg-colored curtains, and showcased the superb silk rug that covered part of the hardwood floor. A delicious warmth emanated from the fire that was lit in the huge brick fireplace. Comfortable, inviting sofas and chairs covered in a pecan-colored fabric surrounded the hearth. Three stemmed wall sconces illuminated the space, and the view to the snow-covered garden was breathtaking. In the distance, Elodie could see a small frozen lake with a white gazebo, and she imagined how pleasant it must be to sit and read there during the warmer months.

Presently, Mrs. Nelson stepped into the room and greeted both women enthusiastically. "I am so glad you came. I'll have lunch served in the small breakfast nook off the kitchen. Let's go and eat before we look at the places I would like you to create arrangements for."

She led Heather and Elodie to a wooden table laden with various delicacies in small Meissen porcelain plates. The nook was cozy, with white wainscoting, ornate crown molding and baseboards that underscored the elegance of the room. The walls were painted in a mist-green color that perfectly complemented the view through the floor-to-ceiling windows.

When they had finished their delicious lunch, Mrs. Nelson showed them the cream-and-peach dining room where the biggest of Elodie's creations would be placed. The white crown molding handsomely set off the walls painted in a soft peach color. The curtains, light peach with dark peach patterns, matched the fabric on the parson chairs. The solid wood table could easily seat twelve people, and two exquisite candle holders were placed slightly off center. The sideboards made of a dark cherry wood beautifully enhanced the room's atmosphere.

"This is the main table. Elodie, I would like you to create a spectacular centerpiece for it. I would also like some decorations for the fireplace mantel in the family room, and some little arrangements to put here and there."

Elodie looked around and tried to capture the ambiance of the rooms, but they felt mostly uninhabited and rather sterile. She asked, "May I take some pictures so I can recall the color scheme of the rooms?"

"Of course, go right ahead," Mrs. Nelson said.

While Elodie took pictures, Heather and Mrs. Nelson returned to the nook and were deep in conversation when Elodie joined them later.

As soon as Heather saw her, she got up and said, "Ready?"

"Yes."

"Then we should head back to the store."

They both thanked Mrs. Nelson for her hospitality, and it was agreed that she would come in by the end of the week to order the flowers.

17

Advent

ADVENT WAS A BUSY time for Elodie, and she worked long hours. The days were short and cold, but she loved being among her colorful friends, the flowers. Creating arrangements took her mind off Mike. Sometimes she could almost feel his presence, but when she turned around, she encountered only empty space. Her heart ached for Mike, and her body yearned for his tender caresses. She could feel the longing awakening in her like flower buds ready to blossom on a clear spring day. But before it went too far, she would throw herself into work and smother the emotions that threatened to overwhelm her.

Despite her vulnerability, Elodie did not allow herself to reveal to the world how much she was suffering. She suspected that Heather had an inkling of what she was feeling but did not confide in her further. Only those who cared to have a closer look at Elodie's floral creations could guess the state of her mind and heart.

This morning, Elodie seemed especially agitated, and her arrangements showed a different twist. They were more stern than playful, the colors subdued rather than vibrant, although still gorgeous.

Heather went over to her and said, "Mrs. Nelson called to say that she will be in this afternoon to choose the flowers for her Christmas decorations. I told her that you would be here."

"That's fine. I'll have lunch in the back room. I brought a sandwich."

As Elodie had already turned back to her work, Heather left her and pensively walked to her office.

Precisely at two o'clock, Mrs. Nelson entered the shop and made her way toward Elodie. "Hi, Elodie," she cheerfully called out, and Elodie greeted her in turn. Heather joined them, and the three women scrutinized some of the arrangements displayed in the vitrine. Elodie made some suggestions regarding color and type of flowers that would be suitable for Mrs. Nelson's home.

"Elodie, please choose the arrangements for me," Mrs. Nelson finally said, "and use the flowers and colors you think would look most spectacular in my house. There are too many choices, and I don't have the eye for it."

"Of course, Elodie answered. "I just need to know how many arrangements you want and how much you want to spend."

"I want a centerpiece in the main dining room, something on the mantelpiece of each fireplace, and a few small, cute things scattered here and there. I'd like the house to feel as if you had just walked into a Christmas wonderland. Can you do this for me, Elodie?"

"Yes. When do you want them at your house? We can deliver them for you."

"Can you have them ready by the twenty-third of December? Oh, and don't worry, money is no object."

Heather, answering for Elodie, said, "We'll deliver them by the twenty-third. I'll give you a call the night before to arrange a convenient time."

"Good," Mrs. Nelson said, then walked out the door.

"You really have impressed her," Heather said to Elodie. "She is absolutely taken with your creations."

"I won't disappoint her. I'll make them the night before they're delivered."

"I think that will be okay if you don't mind working late that day."

Elodie shook her head, and Heather continued, "I have a few more requests from clients that came in this morning." She handed Elodie a list of names and the flowers they had requested.

Elodie looked at the list and shook her head. "Do you realize that some of the flowers they want in the same arrangement don't complement one another, actually quite the opposite? Do you want me to substitute a flower that will be more fitting, or follow their orders?"

"That's a tough question. Some clients may appreciate that, but others might be offended. Let me see whether I know some of them well enough to decide for them. Or maybe I should call them all and make sure there's no special reason why they want a particular flower."

"Good idea," Elodie said, and she continued with the work that gave her the strength she needed to conceal the deep despair of loneliness.

The days leading up to Christmas passed swiftly, and only the dark evenings seemed to drag on. Elodie tried hard to put Mike out of her mind and out of her heart. The former was a lot easier than the latter. So many things reminded her of him. Sometimes she wondered if she should move, but the apartment was very conveniently located, close to her work and to the village. And she was not about to change her life because of a lost love. When the pain became almost physical, she often thought of a sentence she had read somewhere: "Time heals what reason cannot."

So Elodie went through the motions of working, sleeping and eating, and when the twenty-third of December came, all of Mrs. Nelson's arrangements were ready to be delivered. Heather and Elodie packed them into the car and drove to Mrs. Nelson's place. The outside of the house was beautifully decorated, resembling a gift-wrapped parcel. Strings of white lights hung from the pine trees and gave the impression of an enchanted castle.

When they rang the doorbell, the housekeeper opened the door and asked them to place the flowers per Mrs. Nelson's instructions. Heather set the centerpiece on the dining room table, while Elodie arranged the smaller pieces on the fireplace mantels and put the miniature decorations wherever she saw fit. They had just about finished when Mrs. Nelson came home. She inspected the arrangements and their placement and was delighted with what they had done. Handing each woman an envelope, she wished them a merry Christmas.

As it was already late, Heather dropped Elodie off at her apartment and wished her a good night and a wonderful Christmas. When she saw the look on Elodie's face, Heather realized her mistake and muttered an apology. Elodie nodded and got out of the car. With a heavy heart, she climbed the stairs to her apartment, entered and slumped down on her sofa.

"This has to stop," she murmured to herself. "Mike was not my whole life. A big part, but not all of it."

She opened the fridge in search of something to eat and found a half-eaten sandwich, some cheese and her favorite pickles. She poured herself a glass of red wine and sat down in front of the television to consume her lonely meal.

"I need to go away for a few days" she said to herself. "Tomorrow is the last day before Christmas. Heather is visiting friends in Florida, and we'll be closed until the twenty-eighth. That gives me three days to go somewhere."

She turned on the computer and searched the travel sites to find a suitable destination for those three days. Her mind was miles away when she came across a special for Marco Island, the largest of Florida's Ten Thousand Islands. Its tropical, sun-washed, white-sand beaches and easy-paced lifestyle sounded magical and alluring.

"I like this," she said, and she put her itinerary together, selecting a hotel right on the beach. She was about to click the "Purchase" button when her phone started to ring. When she answered, she was surprised to hear Heather's voice.

"Oh, Elodie, thank goodness I caught you. I had to cancel our trip to Florida. My friends there got sick with the flu. So I thought maybe you and I could spend Christmas together?"

"That would be nice," Elodie replied without much conviction.

"Tell you what, we can talk about it in detail tomorrow."

"Okay," Elodie answered, and hung up.

She went back to her computer and signed out of the travel site without booking her trip. She was slightly annoyed at Heather but grudgingly admitted that Heather could not have known of her plans and was kind to propose spending Christmas together. Christmas alone was not much fun, as Elodie well knew from her own experience. She remembered one Christmas in particular, when she was no more than ten years old.

She had been left alone on Christmas Eve while her parents had attended some party in the neighborhood. She had heard them coming home late, shouting at each other, slamming doors. Then she had heard her mother crying. Another door had slammed, then a car had driven away.

It had been the last she had ever heard of her dad. Christmas morning had come and gone, and Elodie had sat alone in the living room, staring at the Christmas tree. There had been no presents for her under the tree, and her mom had not come out of her room until late in the afternoon. When she had finally appeared, she had told Elodie that her dad had left for good and was not coming back.

"And don't you shed a tear for him! He isn't worth it," she had said, going into the kitchen. Elodie had sat there, tears welling up in her eyes, but she had suppressed them and swallowed hard. She could not comprehend why her dad would leave her, but the way her mother had spoken to her, she was afraid to ask. A big black void had started to spread within her, and it had taken all her willpower to get up and go to her room. She had crawled into bed and stared at the ceiling until she had fallen asleep.

Now, why would that sad episode come to mind? Elodie wondered. She did not want to dwell on it, though, and went to the kitchen to make herself a cup of black coffee.

The following day turned out to be one of Elodie's busiest. The arrangements she had created for the holidays sold quickly, and many customers needed more flowers for the next day. When Heather finally closed and locked the door that evening, Elodie was exhausted. She had been on her feet all day with hardly any time for lunch.

"Want to come upstairs for a glass of wine?" Heather asked her.

"Thank you, but I'm done in. I'd rather go home and have a very early night."

"Sleep well and come on over in the afternoon,"

Heather reminded her.

Elodie nodded and walked home. Too tired to cook, she ate a slice of toast with jam and cheese. For once, she took a hot bath and enjoyed soaking in the deep tub with a glass of wine, which made her very sleepy. She got out of the water, dried herself and put on the new pajamas she had ordered from a catalogue. They were soft and warm, and she climbed between the sheets and fell asleep almost immediately.

The next morning, Christmas Day, dawned to a beautiful white world. It was bitter cold, but thankfully, the wind had stopped blowing. Elodie walked to Heather's, where the two women spent a quiet Christmas Day together, drinking red wine and eating all the delicacies Heather had bought at the specialty deli in town. Late in the afternoon, the sky turned an ominous black, and Elodie decided it was time to leave if she wanted to reach her home before the storm broke.

18

The Party

ONE MORNING, Elodie woke up to birds chirping
outside her window and realized that spring had finally
come. Winter had given way to a more temperate season, and the world looked and felt quite different. No
longer was it covered by a white blanket of snow; instead, tender green shoots emerged on trees, and flowers pushed their delicate heads through the dark earth.
Soon, they would erupt in a panoply of colors and delight the nose with their perfume. The breeze was
warm, and the cold winds from the north were forgotten. People walked with a new spring in their step and
smiled more often at passersby. At work, Elodie enjoyed
the different blooms she was given to use in her
creations.

Her arrangements had become more peaceful and
constant, and those who knew how Elodie's work

reflected her emotions might have assumed that she no longer thought of Mike and was going forward with a clear head. They could not have been more mistaken, however. His name still echoed in the black stillness of Elodie's mind, and in the drowsy warmth of her bed, she indulged in her own reveries. But the piercing hurt was gone, and only quiet memories remained.

It was around that time that the elegant Mrs. Nelson came to the store to order some flower bouquets. She invited Elodie and Heather to a party she was giving that weekend in honor of her nephew, who had decided to open his first practice as a medical doctor in town.

When Saturday came, Elodie delivered the flowers to Mrs. Nelson's house and placed them at their intended locations. They looked stunning, and Mrs. Nelson was very pleased. "They look beautiful, as if they were made for this place," she exclaimed, hugging Elodie. "But then I assume you made them for this house, didn't you?"

"Yes," Elodie said simply, "I kept the pictures from Christmas."

Mrs. Nelson nodded and Elodie left. She and Heather would return later for the party.

Back at the store, Heather was waiting for her and told her to go home and dress. "We can meet at Mrs. Nelson's at four o'clock so we'll each have a car and can leave whenever we want," Heather said as she gave Elodie a friendly clap on her shoulder. "Who knows? The young doctor might still be unattached."

Elodie just smiled an enigmatic smile and left. At home, she took a shower and searched through her closet for an appropriate garment to wear to the party. She chose light gray pants and a matching gray blouse, and to add some color, tied a scarf in different hues of blue around her neck. After finding her black Mary Janes and her black clutch, she surveyed herself in the mirror. The gray blouse made her hair appear even blacker, and the blue in the scarf accentuated the gray of her eyes, making them look like the color of the lake on a cloudy day. She put on some burnt-raisin-colored lipstick and was ready to go.

Arriving at the house, she noticed that Heather's car was already there. She rang the doorbell, and the housekeeper let her in and motioned her to follow to the patio, where tables and chairs had been arranged seemingly at random. Elodie spotted Heather at a table and strolled over to her. A waiter brought her a glass of champagne, and she slowly took a sip.

"Do you know anybody here?" she asked Heather.

"A few people who've come to the store lately. Probably acquaintances of Mrs. Nelson's and some folks from the village. I'll introduce them to you when the opportunity arises."

Elodie watched the people mingle. It reminded her of a scene in the movies, the women all decked out in their finest and the men beaming at women who were not their wives. Presently, Mrs. Nelson got up, walked to the wooden podium and announced the arrival of the new doctor.

"I give you Doctor Garter."

A younger man approached her and kissed her hand. "My Aunt Ethel was so kind to introduce me to all of you. As you hopefully know, I'm opening a medical practice in Crystal Grove and hope to see you there when you need a doctor."

He raised his glass and his aunt said, "To your success!"

Everybody raised their glasses and joined in the toast. When the guests were seated again, the waiters began serving appetizers. There were bacon-deviled eggs, red snapper with chilies and sesame, crustless mini tarts, potato croquettes, and blue-crab beignets. Various dips and sauces accompanied these bite-sized delicacies. Elodie had not realized that she was hungry and had to refrain from eating all the deviled eggs.

Before long, the waiters cleared the tables and the dinner service began. Elodie selected the roast tenderloin with Caesar crust, and Heather the spicy lobster pasta. The food was delicious, the wine superb, and Elodie felt happy.

Suddenly, she felt a hand on her shoulder, and a familiar voice said, "Hi, Elodie."

Whirling around, she found herself staring into the gentle brown eyes of Hutch. Elodie gasped and whispered, "Hutch, what in the world are you doing here?"

"Ethel is my aunt. My mother's sister. But what are you doing here?"

Just then, a voice behind them said, "Well, well, I guess you introduced yourself?"

They turned around and saw the friendly face of Hutch's aunt.

"We know one another from our days in Paris,"

answered Hutch.

He took Elodie's hand. "May I have this dance?"

He guided her to the wooden platform that served as a dance floor. The band started to play, and Elodie and Hutch swayed to the rhythm of the song. Gas lanterns had been lit around the perimeter, bathing the garden in an eerie and mystical light. The spring air was still warm from the day's sunshine, and intoxicating scents emanated from the many flowers adorning the garden.

Elodie felt Hutch's arms encircling her and almost imperceptibly caressing her back. She closed her eyes and felt Hutch's embrace tighten as he whispered into her ear, "Where have you been all these years since Paris?"

She slowly opened her gray eyes and murmured, "Lost."

"Oh, Elodie," he breathed into her hair. The touch of his hands was suddenly almost unbearable in its tenderness, and Elodie buried her face against his throat. She could feel his uneven breathing against her cheek and wished they could stay like this forever.

But presently, a slight touch on her arm brought her out of her reverie, and she heard Mrs. Nelson speaking in a low voice. "Hutch, dance with some of the other ladies. You need them if your practice is going to be successful."

Reluctantly, Hutch let go of Elodie and took her back to her table, where Heather was deep in conversation with a gentleman Elodie had seen at the store. When she was seated, the man got up and returned with a glass of white wine for Elodie and red wine for Heather.

He bowed and wished them both a good night.

Heather, looking after him with a thoughtful expression, said, "He was a friend of my husband's and has been coming to the store ever since Frederik passed away. Sometimes I wonder whether he's interested in me or just the store."

When Elodie did not reply, Heather looked at her and said, smiling, "What about you and that very handsome Hutch? How do you know him? I understand he hasn't been in these parts for many years."

"We met in Paris during our college days. We spent a summer at the Sorbonne taking French lessons, and we happened to be in the same classroom," Elodie answered casually. She did not elaborate, and Heather lapsed into silence, leaving her to ponder the twists and turns life takes. She sometimes felt like an innocent pawn in a game whose rules she did not know.

Slowly, the warmth of the day gave way to the chill night air, and Elodie and Heather got up, thanked Mrs. Nelson for a wonderful evening and walked to their cars. As Heather drove off, Elodie lingered for a few moments, savoring the cold air on her hot body, before she, too, drove home. Her mind was filled with pictures of long ago: the first time she had laid eyes on Hutch, the train trip from Paris to Cannes, the nights they had spent at the Hôtel des Orangers, the places and plays they had seen together in Paris, and the last time she had seen Hutch at Charles de Gaulle Airport. She tried to recapture her feelings from that period of her life, but they were elusive, like trying to catch a wave in the ocean.

At least I know now that he's still alive, and with a bit of luck, I'll see him again, she consoled herself, then took a hot bath and went to sleep.

19

A Sunday Drive

ON SUNDAY MORNING, Elodie was awakened by her cell phone ringing. She grabbed it, but it was an unknown number so she did not answer. When it rang again, she put it in the drawer of her nightstand. But it rang again and again until she finally answered.

"Elodie," said a soft male voice, "did I wake you?"

It took her a few moments to recall last night, but when she realized that it was Hutch on the phone, she was instantly wide awake.

"Is that you, Hutch?" she asked.

"Yes, my sleepy one. I need to see you before I go back tomorrow morning to finalize my move here. What about breakfast?"

"Now?" Elodie stammered.

"I'll pick you up in about an hour."

"Okay," Elodie answered. She got out of bed, took a

quick shower and dressed in a flattering white dress with a dark blue wrap, then slipped into her black Mary Janes and grabbed her purse. Elodie eyed her scuffed-up shoes ruefully. They would have to do for today. Contrary to most women, she did not own many pairs of shoes. She always had a hard time finding shoes that fit, and she bought new ones only when the old pair was completely worn out.

When she stepped out the front door, Hutch was leaning against a black Audi Q7, looking tanned and devilishly handsome in his blue jeans, white button-down shirt and black leather jacket. When he saw Elodie, his face broke into a wide grin, and walking up to her, he swept her lightly into his arms. Elodie was completely taken aback, but a small smile of enchantment touched her lips when she caught the faint citrus scent of his after shave.

He twirled her around approvingly. "You look nothing like the girl I knew in Paris," he said. "You're all grown up. But I hope that somewhere in this beautiful woman, I'll still find the girl from Paris."

Elodie couldn't help laughing, and the joyous sound was like pearls of water chasing one another over a rocky river bed. Hutch joined in her laughter, then grew serious and said, "I can't believe it's really you!" He was standing very close, and Elodie thought he might kiss her. Then he moved away, and she wondered if she had imagined that moment. She told herself not to get her hopes up; maybe he didn't have a romantic interest in her, after all, and only thought of her as an old friend.

"Let's go and have breakfast at a little place my aunt

suggested," he said, opening the car door for Elodie. "Apparently, it's well known for its waffles. Do you like waffles?"

"I do, and I haven't had any in ages," Elodie replied.

On the short drive to the breakfast place, they talked about the latest news and the opening of his medical practice in Crystal Grove. Soon, the restaurant's big sign came into view: WAFFLE IRON. After entering, they waited for their eyes to adjust to the semi-darkness inside, then sat down facing each other in a booth located along the far wall. The waitress brought them hot, steaming coffee in tall red mugs while they studied the menu. Elodie ordered a half whole-wheat waffle with pecans and apricot syrup, while Hutch opted for a traditional waffle with maple syrup and whipped cream.

Over breakfast, Elodie recounted how she had ended up in the Midwest. She left out her time with Silvanus, and as Mike was still a sore spot, she decided not to tell Hutch about that part of her life. It could wait. She finished her story just as they put down their knives and forks and took their last sips of coffee. Hutch paid and they left the restaurant.

As they headed back to the car, Hutch asked, "Shall we drive to Moraine Hills Park and walk along the river?"

"That would be lovely," replied Elodie, blushing. Hutch looked at her flushed face but said nothing.

They got into the car and drove off toward McHenry. It was a beautiful late spring day, and the flowers along the road were stretching their colorful heads toward the warming sun. It was the most delightful drive Elodie had taken in a long, long while. Mike's face threatened to intrude, but she quickly turned toward Hutch and studied his profile. She remembered his perfect nose, and she longed to tousle his freshly washed light brown hair, trace the contours of his formidable manly chin and touch his full lips with a soft kiss. Her body slumped into the leather seat, and she sighed deeply.

Hutch turned his head. "Feeling okay?" he asked. His smile was as devastating as ever.

"Oh, yes," Elodie whispered. "It's such a beautiful day for a ride in the country."

She turned her head away from him and stared at the road. Soon they drove through the entrance to the state park, and Hutch parked in one of the many parking lots. He helped Elodie from the car and kept his hold on her hand as they walked toward the nearest trail.

"Any particular way you want to go?" he asked.

Elodie shook her head, and they walked silently through the fresh green of the trees toward the wooden boardwalk winding around the water's edge, where rickety old benches invited passersby to rest for a while. Hutch guided her to a bench shaded by a tall oak tree, and they sat down. He pulled Elodie close to him.

"It seems only yesterday," Hutch said, "that I said good-bye to you in France; and yet, it's been many years. But now, seeing you again, it's as if all those years have melted away. I have this peculiar feeling that I'm living in two parallel worlds."

Elodie looked at him, astonished; although she did not say so, she felt the same way. To her, Hutch had always stayed in the background throughout the years. She had never been able to completely remove him from her life. But she was not prepared to tell him this just yet. Maybe later...if there ever was a later.

For the moment, she asked him, "What have you been up to since then? Obviously, you studied medicine. You must be doing very well, since you're opening your own practice."

"It's a long story. After you boarded that plane, I wasn't quite sure what I wanted to do. Remember, I still had a few weeks left to tour Europe. So I decided to go wherever the tide would take me."

He had taken the bus to the Gare de Lyon, and the first train leaving was headed to Barcelona, the cosmopolitan capital of Spain's Catalonia region; so, to Barcelona he had gone. He had found a cheap hotel close to La Rambla, a popular tree-lined street in central Barcelona, connecting Plaça de Catalunya with the Christopher Columbus Monument at Port Vell. He had visited the maze-like Gothic Quarter and Antoni Gaudí's fantastical Sagrada Família church.

While eating tapas at one of the many little bars tucked away off the main roads, he had noticed a dark-skinned beauty with thick black hair that hung in long, graceful curves over her shoulders, staring at him. She looked ethereal, unreal in the dim light, and he had closed his eyes. When he had opened them again, she had disappeared. Then he had felt a soft touch on his arm and had turned around to find himself gazing into her dark, mysterious eyes. She had motioned him to follow her, and he had obeyed without question. She had led him to a narrow building squeezed between two brightly colored apartment buildings and taken him upstairs. When she had demanded money for services to be rendered, he had realized in horror that he had followed a prostitute to her abode and had fled, dismayed, from her grasp.

"I was so annoyed with myself and the city," Hutch said, "that I left the next morning for Madrid." Elodie was amused at the naiveté of Hutch's younger self but refrained from laughing as he continued his story.

He had stayed in Madrid only a day, long enough to see the exhibitions in the Prado Museum. From there, he had taken the night train to Lisbon, Portugal's hilly capital, and had gone exploring the town. He had climbed to the imposing São Jorge Castle, from where he could see the old city's pastel-colored buildings, as well as Tagus Estuary and the famous suspension bridge. He had spent some days discovering the beaches just outside of Lisbon from Cascais to Estoril, enjoying the sight of the girls sunning themselves on the warm beach; but his adventure in Barcelona had still been fresh in his mind, and he was not interested in repeating the episode.

From Lisbon, he had taken a flight to Italy's ancient capital, Rome, to experience its nearly three thousand years of globally influential art, architecture and culture. He had been awed by St. Peter's Basilica and the masterpieces housed in the Vatican Museums—especially impressive were Michelangelo's Sistine Chapel frescoes—as well as the Colosseum, with its cruel history as an iconic gladiatorial arena, and the Roman

Forum evoking the power of the former Roman Empire. He had spent countless hours walking the cobbled streets of this ancient city and the evenings eating Italian favorites like pasta and pizza in intimate trattorias.

Turning toward Elodie, Hutch said, "Don't I bore you with these old stories?"

"Oh, no," she replied. "I love to hear you talk about all these places I would have liked to go but couldn't. Please go on."

Hutch continued recounting his adventures. From Rome, he had traveled to Florence, one of Italy's most beautiful cities and center of the Renaissance, and had visited the Galleria dell'Accademia to see Michelangelo's *David*, and to the Uffizi Gallery to see Botticelli's *The Birth of Venus* and da Vinci's *Annunciation*. After Florence, he had gone to Venice, a city built on more than one hundred islands in a marshy lagoon in the Adriatic Sea, and had been astounded to learn that there were no cars or roadways, just boats and canals. He had toured the sights by day and spent the evenings sitting at La Piazza San Marco, drinking prosecco produced in the Veneto region and watching the crowds stroll by.

As summer gave way to fall, Hutch had taken the train to Vienna, where he had found a job as an English teacher in one of the many schools. He had rented a small apartment close to the school and taught there for one semester, filling in for the regular teacher, who had taken a sabbatical to go abroad and research a theological question. Hutch had liked teaching but did not envision doing it for a living.

Shortly before Christmas, the semester had ended, and he had traveled south to Athens, Greece, one of the oldest cities in the world, and had spent his days visiting the famous ruins of antiquity and eating at street food stands, sleeping in a hostel at night. When the weather had turned cold, he had realized it was time to go back to the US.

"And that's the story of my travels in Europe," he said. "I would have liked to visit the Scandinavian countries and, above all, Russia, but it was too cold, and I was low on financial reserves. My parents were thrilled when I called to tell them I was coming home. They picked me up at the airport in Seattle and organized a family reunion for the following weekend. I must say that I was happy to be back in the good old USA."

"I wish I had been able to see all the places you have, but I had to go back as my finances were in bad shape," Elodie said with a sigh. "But hopefully, one day I'll be able to travel through Europe."

"We can travel together. I would love to go back to the old country," Hutch said, and he gently took Elodie's hand in his. Surprised, Elodie looked up at him and met his serenely compelling eyes. She acutely felt his nearness, and it made her head spin. Her thoughts raced back to the day she had met him. And yet, she heard a mocking voice inside, wondering if he could be baiting her. Abruptly, she got up and started to walk toward the parking lot.

Hutch followed her immediately and took her by the shoulders. "Did I say something to upset you?" he

asked, puzzled, his eyes mirroring his inner turmoil.
Elodie shook her head and kept on walking. When
they got to the car, Elodie turned and faced Hutch.
"Please take me home," she said. "All that talk of
faraway places has made me tired."

Hutch, noticing her pale, pinched face, got into the
car without a word and maneuvered out of the parking
lot and onto the road toward Crystal Grove.

When they arrived at her place, she said, "Don't
bother coming to the door; I'll be fine. Thank you for a
lovely day." And she disappeared inside her building.
She laboriously walked up the stairs and entered her
apartment. Ever so slowly, she took off her shoes and
slumped onto her sofa. She was exhausted and sensu-
ally disturbed, unable to keep her thoughts together.
With great difficulty, she dragged herself to her bed.
Her whole body was engulfed in waves of fatigue and
despair.

Sleep was long in coming, but when it finally did, it
was calm and restoring. When the morning sun shone
through the window, Elodie woke up feeling refreshed.
She remembered having had these episodes before.
They had always left her inescapably tired, but after a
long night's rest, she would feel just fine. She did not
quite know what brought this weariness about, only
that it had to do with her emotions. She wondered why
being with Hutch had affected her so but decided not to
dwell on it.

"Maybe if I'm lucky, he'll call and I can explain," she
mused.

20

Mrs. Nelson

AS SUMMER TURNED into fall and Elodie did not hear from Hutch again, she resolved with a heavy heart to put him out of her mind for good. She went to work every day and created her flower arrangements, which underwent a subtle change; they were serene, less playful, and the color palette she selected was more subdued. The customers, as well as Heather, liked the new look. Heather had expanded the storefront, and now Elodie's arrangements were prominently displayed in the cooled window vitrine. This led to even more orders for Elodie's arrangements, and Heather's store flourished.

One day, when Elodie arrived at work, she found Heather in the shop waiting for her. "Elodie, I have bad news. Mrs. Nelson has had a stroke and is in the hospital."

"When did it happen? How is she?" Elodie asked, concerned.

"It happened the day before yesterday. They took her to the hospital, and her nephew is attending her."

"Oh," was all that came over Elodie's lips, and a shadow clouded her eyes.

"Let's go and visit her tonight," Heather said, "and see if she needs anything."

"I can't," Elodie said, and she turned around to leave.

"Is it because of her nephew?"

Elodie spun around and looked Heather in the eye. "What do you mean?"

"Oh, Elodie, I know you like Hutch, and I also know that he hasn't been to see you lately, but do this for a lonely, elderly lady. I know that Mrs. Nelson would be so pleased to see you. She has often spoken of you and your special touch with flowers."

Elodie looked confused, so Heather continued, "We have become very close since the party, and I have dined at her house almost every week."

"Well," Elodie said, unconvinced, "if you think I should, then I'll come with you."

After work, the two women drove to the hospital. When they entered Mrs. Nelson's room, they were shocked at what they saw. Mrs. Nelson was lying in a bed that seemed much too big for her frail body. Her face was chalk white and her thin lips colorless. Her lifeless eyes were staring at the white ceiling, and she did not move or blink when they approached the bed.

Heather slowly took the small hand into hers. "How

are you, my dear friend?" she whispered. But the figure in the bed did not answer, and tears slowly trickled down Heather's cheeks.

A nurse came in and asked to speak to them privately. Outside the room, she told them that there was not much hope of Mrs. Nelson's recovery. She had sustained substantial brain damage, and even if she were to regain consciousness, she would never be able to return home and would have to spend the rest of her life in a nursing home, confined to a wheelchair.

Heather took Elodie's arm, and slowly they walked out of the hospital.

"I can't believe it!" Heather said. "A few days ago, she was just fine. We had made plans to go shopping in the city, and she was very much looking forward to that. Oh, Elodie! We are so incredibly fragile, and life can be snatched from us in a heartbeat."

Heather fell silent, and Elodie helped her into the car, then drove to the shop. She walked with her upstairs and stayed a while. Heather was just sitting in the chair facing the garden, deep in thought, when the phone rang. Elodie answered and was shocked into silence; Hutch was on the other end, asking for Heather.

"One moment, please," she whispered.

She handed the receiver to Heather, who looked at her questioningly. "Who is it?"

"It's her nephew."

Heather took the receiver and listened; then she hung up, her face ashen, and gave Elodie the news. "She took a turn for the worse and closed her eyes forever soon after we left her."

Elodie went to Heather and hugged her. "I am so sorry, Heather. If there is anything I can do, please let me know."

Heather shook her head and said, "I want to be alone now. I'll be okay."

Elodie saw the determination in Heather's eyes, nodded and left. When she arrived home, a black car was parked in front of her apartment building. She had just opened the front door when a muted voice behind her said, "Elodie."

She turned around and there was Hutch, his eyes filled with deep sadness.

"Come upstairs," she said, taking his hand. He followed her automatically and sat down on the sofa.

"I just heard about your aunt," Elodie said. "I am terribly sorry for your loss."

"She seemed to be getting better, but then suddenly, her body started to shut down, and before we could do anything she passed away."

As Hutch stared into the void, Elodie noiselessly went to the kitchen to make some coffee. She put a steaming cup in front of him, and he gladly took a sip.

"I owe you an apology for not getting in touch with you after we last saw each other. When I got back that night, I had a message from my lawyer that it was imperative I meet him on Monday. You see, I was in the middle of a messy divorce. I didn't mention it to you because, well—I wanted to get that over and done with and be free of her before reconnecting with you."

Elodie smiled at him and gently pressed his hand.

"Ethel, my aunt, has been very kind and helpful to me during this time, and I was looking forward to spending time with her. But now, I shall never be able to tell her how much she meant to me."

Elodie could feel his distress and put her arm around his shoulder.

"I have to go," Hutch said, getting up. "I'll call you later in the week."

When Hutch closed the door behind him, Elodie's whole being seemed to be filled with waiting. She walked to the window, and as she watched him drive away, a silent prayer left her lips: *Come back to me, Hutch.*

As if he had heard her, the black car turned and came back, and Elodie watched in surprise as Hutch got out. Before he could even ring the doorbell, she had opened the door for him. Without a word, he swept her, weightless, into his arms. Her calm was shattered by the hunger of his kisses, and she returned them with unrestrained abandon. They sank down on the soft rug in front of the fireplace, and Hutch hurriedly undressed her and then threw his clothes on a pile beside them, all the while caressing Elodie's body. His touch light and painfully teasing, and she instinctively arched toward him. There was no time to explore each other's bodies, and she gasped as he lowered his body onto hers. When he kissed her taut nipples before entering her, a melting sweetness arose within her, and she yielded to the searing need that had been building for months.

Afterwards, with their passion spent, they each

retreated into their own worlds. Lazily, they got up and dressed, and he brushed a gentle kiss on her waiting lips, leaving her mouth burning with fire.

"I'll be back tomorrow evening," he said as he departed reluctantly.

Elodie sat down on her sofa, feeling as light as air. The ghosts of the past that had been haunting her had been driven away, at least temporarily, by Hutch's gentle caresses and soft kisses, still so vivid in her memory. She wondered if Hutch would come back as he had promised.

"I must wait and see," she whispered to her reflection as she passed the mirror on the way to her room. She went to bed feeling satisfied and full of hope.

The morning sun woke Elodie with a warm kiss, and she stretched like a kitten, still feeling euphoric. She closed her eyes again, trying to recapture the intense moments of last night. A smile spread over her face as she slowly crawled out of bed and took a long, hot shower.

When she got to the store, she found Heather, dressed in mourning, trying to put together some flowers. She gently led her to a chair and took the flowers from her hands. Deftly, she created a beautiful arrangement for Heather to take to Ethel's house.

"Please come with me, Elodie; I can't go on my own. I need you to lean on," Heather whispered, her voice filled with tears.

"Of course," Elodie replied, even though she did not want to go. "When do you want to leave?"

"After we close the store tonight."

Heather went back to her office, and Elodie busied herself with ordering flowers, putting the new arrivals in buckets with water, and making a few more summer arrangements. The day passed quickly, and after the last customer had gone, she closed the store and went in search of Heather. She found her in her apartment, sitting in the chair contemplating the backyard full of tall trees, their thick trunks surrounded by blooming hosta plants.

When she heard Elodie come in, Heather got out of her chair and grabbed her purse. "I'm ready to go," she said.

Silently, both women descended the stairs. Elodie fetched the flowers and opened the car door for Heather. After a short drive, they arrived at Ethel's house and walked to the front door. It was open, and pieces of conversation floated out into the garden.

"I'll wait here for you," Elodie said, then turned to sit down on one of the chairs beside the walkway.

"I won't be long," Heather responded, and she entered the house.

For a while, Elodie tried to understand what the conversations were all about, but she soon gave up and watched the day giving way to night. It was a warm evening; the air was scented with the sweet smell of flowers, and Elodie was transported back to Cannes, when she and Hutch had searched for a place to have dinner in the mild Mediterranean air filled with the scent of flowers. She closed her eyes and a smile crossed her face.

Suddenly, angry voices interrupted her reverie, and

when she turned to find the source, she saw Hutch and a woman having a bitter argument. "Go, and never come back again. I don't want to ever see you again in this life!" she heard Hutch shout, but could not catch what the woman replied. A car door slammed and tires screeched as a white car left the parking lot.

Then Hutch appeared and seemed stunned to find Elodie sitting on the lawn chair. "What are you doing here?" he asked.

"I brought Heather over and decided to wait out here."

"Please come in," he said, taking her arm; but when they reached the door, Heather came out, and Elodie took her arm and nodded farewell to Hutch.

As they were driving back to the store, Heather said, "Did you see that woman shouting? That was Hutch's ex-wife. Ethel told me the whole sordid story about them. They got married only a couple of years ago, and almost immediately the whole thing fell apart. She wanted a glamorous life with everything—jewelry, vacations in exotic places, a huge house decorated by famous interior designers and so on. You get the picture, no? She was unwilling to wait until they could afford it and started an affair with a playboy from New York. Hutch soon found out and started divorce proceedings. As you can imagine, love had already turned into hate, and the divorce was finalized last week. I have not a clue why she turned up here, but Hutch is pretty upset about it and asked her to leave."

Before Elodie could answer, they arrived at the store, and Heather got out of the car, thanking her for the ride.

"See you tomorrow," Elodie said.

She drove home and slowly went up the stairs to her apartment. Jumbled thoughts raced in her head, and she wondered if Hutch would confide in her about his ex-wife. She had hardly put down her purse when the doorbell rang. It was Hutch.

"Come in," she said, holding the door open for him.

"I have to talk to you if you have time," he said.

"Sit down and I'll make you a cup of coffee. Then we can talk."

When they were seated with their coffee mugs in front of them, Hutch started to speak. He had met Sandra at a gala charity event in New York some three years ago. She was a flamboyant, blond, extremely beautiful young woman, and all the men vied for her attention. Somehow, she had picked Hutch to be her escort for the evening, and not long thereafter, they had started dating. At first, it was like a dream. Sandra was easygoing, playful and always ready for adventure.

After six months, Hutch proposed and Sandra became his wife. Almost from one day to the next, she changed completely. She became demanding and difficult—nothing was good enough for her. Hutch tried to please her, to no avail. They fought almost constantly, and the stress this caused had made Hutch's life miserable.

When he refused to buy a penthouse in Manhattan that she had found and wanted, things became worse. She bought expensive jewelry and designer clothes on credit until Hutch canceled her credit cards. She was

furious and started an affair with a notorious woman-
izer. That had been the last straw for Hutch. He moved
out of the rented apartment and started divorce proceedings. It was very messy. She had tried to get a per-
centage of Hutch's future earnings, but the judge had
not been blinded by her and had left her with nothing,
not even alimony.

"Three weeks ago, the divorce became final, and now
I'm free of her. Ethel and I were going to celebrate, but
now..."

Elodie took his hand in hers and stroked the long,
elegant fingers. He stared straight ahead, unseeing.
Elodie sat quietly, waiting for him to find his way back
to the present.

After what seemed like an endless string of empty
minutes, Hutch moved. His eyes lost their empty look,
and he clasped Elodie's hand. "That's the story of my
marriage in a nutshell. It was hell, and I'm grateful it's
over for good. At least the divorce was finalized while
my aunt was still alive."

"What are your plans for the future?"

"I'll open the practice as planned and settle here in
Crystal Grove. If you have time and feel like it, will you
help me?"

Elodie swallowed hard and whispered, "Of course.
Just tell me what you want me to do."

"If you have nothing planned tomorrow evening, I
can show you the place. I'd like to know what you think
of it."

"That would be lovely."

Hutch got up, gently pulled Elodie to her feet and

pressed his masculine body against hers. His arms encircled her, and he brushed a gentle kiss across her forehead. "I have to go back. I'll see you tomorrow evening."

He let go of her and headed toward the door. She needed all her resolve not to run after him, so intense were her feelings for him at that moment. When the door closed behind him, Elodie ran to the window and watched him drive away.

"Hutch," she whispered, "if this is just a game to you, I don't know whether I'll be able to recover after it's over. I hid my love for you once before, but this time, I'm not sure I can do it again."

She watched television for a while, but nothing caught her fancy, so she tried to read in bed. However, she was unable to concentrate on the story. The inner turmoil of her emotions was wreaking havoc on her mind. She turned off the bedside lamp and tried to sleep, but sleep would not come, and she tossed and turned. Finally, she fell asleep and had such a vivid dream about being with Hutch in Paris that when she awoke in the early morning hours, it took her a moment to realize that she was in Crystal Grove, and that many years had passed since she had been that young girl in Paris.

At work, the intense feeling of Hutch's presence lingered all day. The anticipation of seeing Hutch that evening and the fear that he might not come made the day unbearable. She immersed herself in creating flower arrangements and was glad when it was evening and she could go home.

Turning the corner to her apartment, she saw his black car parked at the curb and almost ran to him. As soon as he caught sight of her, he got out of the car, came toward her, and kissed her cheek. Arm in arm, they climbed the stairs to her apartment.

"Let's go to the office first," he said, then added with a teasing smile, "If I stay here another minute with you, I can't guarantee I'll behave like a gentleman."

"Let's go," Elodie replied. *And play later,* she thought.

It was a short drive to the office located on the south side of town. The two-story redbrick building, with its tall windows and small white balconies projecting gracefully into the air, stood proudly among gnarled old trees in a pretty park. Hutch unlocked the heavy wooden door, and they entered a small hallway with several doors that led to different rooms. To the right was a welcoming waiting room with comfortable chairs arranged along the walls. On one wall was a large magazine rack that held colorful magazines and a selection of newspapers. The reception area was hidden behind a high counter, where the patients would sign in. Behind that was a tiny, fully equipped kitchen, a conference room and filing cabinets. A door led from the waiting room to a second hallway adjacent to the reception area and to the examination rooms. While they inspected the premises, Hutch told her about the different machines and their uses, and the number of employees he had already hired. He was hoping to open the practice by the end of October.

"It looks to me as if you're ready to open for business

tomorrow. Everything seems to be all set," Elodie said.

"I guess I could, but I need a few weeks to prepare myself for the life of a country doctor." He smiled. "And I had hoped that you and I could go away together for a few days. What do you think?"

Elodie was taken by surprise. She had not thought that far ahead and was still unsure about her relationship with Hutch. Was he genuinely interested in her, or did he see her as the friend from their long-ago student days?

Hutch noticed the change in her expression and looked at her with gentle amusement. "Let's go to your place and we'll talk. I guess I've made quite a few assumptions, even though I know very well that assumptions often lead to trouble." He took Elodie's arm, guided her out of the office and locked the door.

On the way back to Elodie's place, they picked up some food from a little Chinese restaurant not far from her apartment. They put the takeout containers on the coffee table, turned on the television and watched a sitcom while they ate the delicious meal. After clearing away the leftovers, Elodie made coffee, and they watched the end of the program. Hutch seemed to have forgotten his earlier promise to talk about their relationship. Elodie wondered if she should bring it up herself but decided against it, resigning herself to waiting a little longer to be released from her uncertainty.

After a while, Hutch checked his watch and exclaimed, "It's late, and I have an early appointment at the hospital. May I see you tomorrow night? We can talk about a little getaway then."

Elodie nodded, and Hutch took his leather jacket from the closet, kissed her lightly on the cheek and was gone before Elodie had said good night.

21

A Special Trip

THE NEXT DAY dragged on, and Elodie kept herself busy creating flower arrangements for the vitrine and, later, ordering new flowers from her suppliers. Time and time again, she found herself thinking of the get-away Hutch had suggested. She did not want to dwell on it, but the thought kept intruding.

Maybe it was only words he spoke. Maybe he didn't mean it, she admonished herself. When you loved someone, she wondered, why did their smallest actions or words have such an impact on your psyche? When it was finally closing time, she wished everybody a good evening and walked home, deep in thought.

She had hardly put her purse down when the doorbell rang, and Hutch impatiently entered with a big smile on his face. "The hospital has accepted me as a surgeon on their staff," he almost shouted. He grabbed

Elodie around the waist and spun her around, his eyes filled with merriment and eagerness. "Now I'm really looking forward to opening my practice here."

Elodie smiled; at this moment, he reminded her so much of the young student she had known in Paris, when they were both filled with the wonders of the world they were going to explore.

"What are you thinking about?" he asked, and Elodie just shrugged her shoulders.

"Our days in Paris," she answered.

"It seems like such a long time ago. So much has happened to both of us since then, but I believe we can recapture the spirit of those days. Are you willing to try?"

"I am if you are," she replied.

"Agreed! Let's go and have dinner at that little diner; I'm starving. I only had a cup of coffee this morning." So, hand in hand, they walked to the diner.

Later, back at her apartment, Elodie was still not quite convinced about Hutch's intentions and decided to wait and see what the next few weeks would bring. Hutch, oblivious to her doubts, pulled out his tablet and showed her places they could escape to and enjoy the last days of summer. To Elodie, they were all lovely with their deep, azure-blue waters and white sandy beaches lined with palm trees.

"Any one of these places is fine with me," she said. "I haven't been to any of them, and they all look so inviting."

"What do you think of Key West? It's not that far, and it's quite an amusing place to stay."

"Agreed." Elodie smiled.

Hutch checked available flights and hotels, then asked, "Will the weekend after next work for you?"

"I think so. I'll talk to Heather tomorrow and make sure."

"Let's call her now. It's only eight o'clock."

Elodie called Heather, who was happy for her and told her to take the whole week off. When Elodie relayed what Heather had said, Hutch grinned but refrained from commenting. They booked the flight for Tuesday, with a return flight on Saturday, and made reservations at an inn off the main street.

"This will be so much fun!" Hutch said. "Like the trip we took to Cannes. Do you remember?"

How could she not remember? It had been one of the most wonderful weekends she had ever had. She answered, "Of course I remember. We stayed at that old hotel with the colorful bathroom not far from the harbor."

"And we had dinner at that Moroccan restaurant by the Mediterranean Sea. Ah, Elodie, I am so glad that destiny brought us together again."

He stood up and pulled her gently toward him. She was conscious of where his warm flesh touched hers, making her skin tingle. His slow, drugging kiss sent shivers of ecstasy through her entire body. Shocked at her own eager response to the touch of his lips, she buried her face against his throat and tried to regain her composure.

Reluctantly, he released her. "I have to be away for a few days," he said, "but I will be back Monday with my bags packed for Florida. I'll pick you up Monday evening, and we can spend the night at an airport hotel. It will be more convenient than having to leave here at the crack of dawn and battle traffic on Interstate 90."

"I shall be ready," she said with a smile.

The next several days flew by, and suddenly, it was Sunday morning. Elodie stayed a bit longer in bed and reflected on the past weeks with Hutch. She remembered the intimacy of his kisses and wondered what the future would bring. She still did not dare to completely believe that he would not abandon her. He was like a butterfly: a taste here and a taste there. At least, that was Elodie's assessment of him.

On Monday evening, Hutch's black Audi stopped at the curb, and she ran downstairs to meet him. He put her bag in the trunk, then opened the door for her. His lips brushed against hers, and there was a sparkle of mischief in his eyes. Elodie ignored it but was startled by the delicious sensation of his lips touching hers. She hastily averted her eyes and busied herself getting into the car.

Hutch drove fast, concentrating on the road and traffic ahead. Soon they reached the interstate, and the rush-hour traffic grew heavier as they got closer to the airport.

"I've booked a room at the Hilton Airport hotel. It will make it easier to get to our flight tomorrow," he said, and Elodie agreed.

She wondered what he expected from her that night, and it made her slightly uncomfortable. She did not want to appear too easy, but neither did she want to seem a prude. *I guess I'll leave it up to him to take the lead,* she thought. She sighed.

"Are you all right?" he asked, concerned.

"Yes, I'm fine."

When they arrived at the airport, Hutch parked the car, and they walked the few steps to the Hilton's spacious lobby and checked in. A tired-looking bellboy brought their bags to the room. Then Hutch suggested eating at Andiamo, an Italian restaurant located in the hotel, and they had a tasty dinner of spaghetti and meatballs.

Back in the room, Elodie was surprised to see the table covered with a white tablecloth, a bottle of champagne resting in a wine cooler, and two tall champagne glasses waiting to be filled. Small porcelain plates held a selection of colorful desserts: delicate fruit tarts, cups with custard and berries, tiny cream-filled Neapolitans, bite-sized brownies and soft crepes.

Before Elodie could react, Hutch came up behind her and drew her to him, whispering into her ear, "I don't ever want to lose you again."

Gently, ever so gently, he unbuttoned her blouse and let it drop to the floor. His touch provoked a passion she had thought lost, and it inflamed her whole body. Softly, he pressed her onto the king-sized bed and slowly pulled off her jeans. His fingers unhooked her bra, and his burning lips touched her hardened nipples with tantalizing possessiveness. The gentle touch sent currents of desire through her, and she pulled him to her, trying to unbutton his shirt. Hutch hurriedly stepped out of his clothes, and the sleek caress of his body electrified her. Relentlessly, his hands moved downward on either side of her body, exploring her hips, waist and thighs, until finally he removed her panties.

For a moment, Elodie felt vulnerable, as if he was shattering the hard shell she had built so carefully. Then his lips recaptured hers, more demanding this time, sending spirals of ecstasy through her. His body moved to cover hers, imprisoning it in a web of intensifying arousal. She cried out for release, and they both exploded in a downpour of fiery sensations. She savored the feeling of satisfaction that engulfed her and knew that she would allow him to tear apart her soul.

Later, they both slipped into the soft bathrobes provided by the hotel. Hutch served the chilled champagne, and they toasted each other. In a hushed voice, Hutch said, "I love you, and I will love you all the days of my life." He kissed her gently on her waiting lips. They both felt at peace, and tonight, there were no shadows across Elodie's heart.

The next morning, they boarded a flight to Miami. Once they had landed, they picked up their rental car and drove south on US Route 1, the Overseas Highway, toward Key West. As they drove, Hutch explained that large parts of this over one-hundred-mile-long highway had been built on the former right-of-way of the Florida East Coast Railway's Overseas Railroad.

"The Key West Extension of the railway was completed in 1912, but it was destroyed by the Labor Day hurricane of 1935. The company didn't have the money to rebuild, so they sold the roadbed and remaining bridges to the state of Florida. It was then that this road was built. Now you know," he said, smiling, while concentrating on the heavy traffic.

"How do you know so much about this?" Elodie asked.

"I was interested in finding spectacular drives in the US, and Miami to Key West was listed in some catalogue as a great American road trip."

As they traveled through the fabled Florida Keys, Elodie concentrated on the spectacular view out her window. The road was surrounded on both sides by water, which was sometimes obscured by small villages and abundant vegetation. When they came to the famous Seven Mile Bridge stretching out into the open sea, Elodie caught her breath in awe at the sight. Her anticipation grew as they drew closer to the island city of Key West, which Hutch had told her was a refuge to writers and artists.

Elodie was enjoying the drive immensely but occasionally stole a glance at Hutch. Her feelings for him had been newly awakened last night, and she knew that she had reached the point of no return. She wanted very much to forever journey with him through life. She remembered what he had said last night about loving her always and hoped that he had meant that he would stay with her always, but was afraid to believe it. She did not want to get hurt again.

While her thoughts chased one another, Hutch drove confidently on, and after a short three hours, they arrived at their bed-and-breakfast in historic Old Town Key West, where Duval Street meets the Atlantic Ocean.

Their room faced toward the ocean, and Elodie stepped out onto the balcony and gazed over the iridescent waters. No clouds obscured the deep blue sky, and a soft wind ruffled the fronds of the palms standing guard at the water's edge. The air was filled with the scent of flowers and a slight hint of seawater.

Hutch came up behind Elodie and put his strong arms around her, whispering in her ear, "Do you like it here?"

"It's one of the most beautiful places I've ever been to," she replied with a smile in her voice, "and it's you that makes it so special."

Hutch turned her to face him and gently kissed her waiting lips. "Let's go and find something to eat, and then we can relax at the beach or by the pool."

So off they went in search of food. Tantalizing smells wafted through the air from the many little cafes and bistros lining the streets. Finally, they settled on fish-and-chips. The fish was crisp, the fries freshly made and the tartar sauce divine. After they had finished the last bite, they strolled along Duval Street, stopping here and there to look at the pretty window displays.

The street was crowded, and as it was still hot, they decided to go for a quick swim in the ocean. It felt good to be immersed in the cool seawater up to their necks. They swam for a little while, then returned to the hotel. Hutch went for a dive in the pool, but Elodie was tired and went to their room.

It was a beautifully appointed room, with an upholstered headboard in a warm coffee color. The bedding was white and simple, contrasting nicely with the light bed frame and complementing the dark walls. Linen curtains in various hues of blue and green framed the large windows, and a soft, dark carpet covered the floor.

Elodie went out onto the balcony and looked out over the calm turquoise sea. She tried to tell herself that she was happy, but she felt deep inside her that something was marring an otherwise perfect day. However, she was unable to put her finger on it, and with a sigh, she turned and stepped back into the room just as Hutch came through the door.

"Are you all right?" he asked, concerned. "I heard you sigh."

"I'm fine," she lied, concealing her uneasiness with a smile.

Hutch nodded, then disappeared into the shower, and she heard the water being turned on. She sat down on one of the soft chairs with her legs pulled up under her. To chase the uninvited thoughts away, she turned on the television and watched the weather channel. The forecast called for some rain during the night but sunshine the next day.

Soon, Hutch emerged from the bathroom, walked out on the balcony and leaned against the railing, looking out over the still water. Elodie watched him admiringly. He had a remarkable physique with his broad shoulders, powerful arms and straight legs. He held his head high, and his open shirt revealed a muscular chest covered with crisp blond hair that Elodie found irresistible. She felt the urge to run to him and press her body to his. But before she could get up,

Hutch came back into the room.

"Do you want to go out for a night on the town," he asked, "or shall we have room service bring up a bottle of wine and some snacks?"

"I like the idea of room service. I'm tired from the flight, and all the walking and swimming."

Hutch ordered chicken wings, burger sliders, sweet potato fries with ketchup and ranch sauce, and a bottle of sauvignon blanc. It did not take long for the waiter to arrive with the food and set it on the small table on the balcony. They savored the young wine, nibbled on the curly fries and chicken wings and ate the delicious burgers. While they were busy eating and talking, the sun slowly started to descend, setting the western sky aflame. They watched until it dropped into the calm water and disappeared. Darkness chased away the sun's last rays, and Hutch reached for Elodie's hand.

Slowly, they got up and went inside. On the mantelpiece were some candles, and Hutch lit one after the other, filling the room with the warm glow of candlelight and the scent of persimmons and mint. Elodie approached Hutch from behind and wound her arms around his body, leaning gently against him. Hutch turned and kissed first the tip of her nose, then her eyes, and finally, her soft mouth. Her knees weakened as he gently led her to the bed and eased her down like a feather. His mouth found her lips again and smothered them with exquisite mastery. She responded with eagerness, shivering at the sweet tenderness of his kisses. Safe in the arms of this man, she savored every second of their intimacy.

When he began to undress her, she felt no guilt but floated on a cloud of contentment. She snuggled against him, their legs intertwined, and caressed his muscular back. She felt his passion being aroused and welcomed him into her. Together they found the rhythm that bound their bodies together. The turbulence of passion raged through them both and exploded in a torrent of blazing sensations. Serenity and harmony flowed between them as they succumbed to the numbed sleep of satisfied lovers.

Bright sunshine woke Elodie the next morning. Hutch was sitting on the balcony drinking strong black coffee. She sheepishly snuck up behind him and kissed him on the head.

"Come here," he said, pulling her into his lap. "Want some coffee?"

"No, thank you, but I'll have some orange juice." He poured her a tall glass of freshly squeezed orange juice, and she drank it thirstily.

"How would you like to rent a scooter and explore the town and its surroundings?"

"Sounds like fun," Elodie answered. She put the glass down on the small table. "I'll take a quick shower and then we can go."

Watching her disappear, Hutch wondered what life had been like for her since they had parted in Paris all those many years ago. Then she had been easygoing, innocent and filled with wonder, but he had not known her well enough, he admitted to himself. And now, he only knew that he did not want to let her go ever again.

After she had showered and dressed, she called to

Hutch from the bedroom, and he got up and joined her. Together they went down to the lobby to inquire where they might find a scooter rental office.

"It's right across from here, on the other side of the street," the friendly man at reception replied.

So they stepped out into the sunshine, crossed the busy street and rented a yellow scooter for the day. They rode up and down the streets of downtown Key West, then ventured out along the beach until they saw a stand selling cold beer, juices and bottled water. They stopped and drank the cold beverages in big gulps.

"That felt good," Elodie said, and Hutch agreed.

"I'd like to see where Ernest Hemingway lived," he said, and Elodie nodded.

"I've read several of his books, and I absolutely adore them," she replied.

After a few wrong turns, they eventually arrived at the grand home of Hemingway, with its vintage attractiveness and aging beauty. They strolled through the extensive gardens with its sanctuary for cats, then entered through the main door of the two-story house, whose tall windows gave it an air of sophistication. In one of the great rooms, a three-seat sofa was eminently stationed with its back against the windows overlooking the lush, green tropical gardens. Elodie thought the sofa—carmine-red plush with light polka dots and embedded buttons, mounted on a dark-brown wooden frame—gave the room a cheery atmosphere. On each side of the sofa, potted ferns in dark urns endured endless visitors drifting through the house, and tall candle holders stood at attention. After wandering around for a couple of hours, Hutch and Elodie left the house and went in search of a place to have dinner.

In one of the side streets, they found a quaint restaurant offering outdoor seating and made a reservation, deciding to return the scooter first and later return to the restaurant. After a quick swim in the pool and a shower, they dressed and ambled back to the restaurant. By now, the lights were coming on, and when they turned the corner, they were enchanted to see sparkling lights draped around the stately oak trees, and miniature lamps hanging from the feathery bushes. The old iron lanterns were lit, bathing the patio in a soft glow. A friendly server led them to their reserved table at the edge of the patio, close to the murmuring water fountain. They ate their dinner—pink shrimp with a variety of sauces, and a slice of the famous key lime pie for dessert—with pleasure, hungry as they were after a day spent riding on a scooter.

The night was warm, and a lazy breeze was blowing through the palm fronds, making them sing their own special song. They walked arm in arm back to the hotel. Elodie was tired but happy, and she glanced up to see Hutch looking at her sidewise.

"I love you, Elodie," he said. He turned her to him, his hand cupping her face gently. "I want to be with you always. Will you marry me?"

Elodie was stunned. She had known that she was hopelessly in love with this gorgeous man but had not dared believe that he might return her love.

"Yes," she said. She felt her blood coursing through her veins like a raging river. Standing on tiptoe, she kissed him on his waiting lips.

"Elodie, tonight you make me the happiest man under the stars. I promise you won't ever lack for anything, and I will be true to you always."

Elodie looked into his face, radiant with joy. Inside her, something shifted—it was the little box where the memory of Mike resided. It had moved further away, and she was no longer affected by the hurt and pain he had caused. Only happiness and contentment filled her.

Hutch kissed her. He said, with a slight tinge of wonder in his voice, "Let's go back to the hotel and make some plans."

To celebrate their engagement, they had room service bring them a bottle of Dom Pérignon. They talked, laughed and drank champagne until midnight.

"We should sleep," Hutch said at last. "We have to be on the road by eight o'clock."

"That's fine with me. I'm sleepy, too," Elodie said with a smile playing around her mouth.

They fell asleep at once, and all too soon it was morning and time to get up. After a quick breakfast, they drove back to Miami and boarded an afternoon flight for Chicago. They arrived on time at O'Hare, retrieved the car and drove straight to Crystal Grove.

When they pulled up outside Elodie's place, Hutch walked her to her door. "I'll come by tomorrow evening," he said, and he brushed his lips against hers. "Have a good night."

Elodie watched him drive away, then slowly mounted the stairs to her apartment. She put her bag on the floor, got a bottle of water from the fridge and sat down on her favorite chair. Thoughts chased one another like silver raindrops in a rusty rain gutter.

22

The Grand Opening

THE WEATHER WAS still mild, although the days had perceptibly shortened and darkness came early. Elodie and Hutch spent every free minute together, going over the many details that still needed their attention. Hutch wanted to open his practice on November 1 and had invited his parents and many of his relatives and friends to the event. At that time, he planned to announce that he and Elodie would be married on Christmas Day.

By the end of October, Hutch's new offices were ready for the opening. The furniture had been delivered and arranged, his medical instruments put in their proper places and the support staff hired. Elodie and Hutch walked one more time through the rooms, arranging a chair here, closing a drawer there.

"It looks inviting," Elodie said, "even though it is a

doctor's office."

"What do you mean?" Hutch asked, irritated.

"Just that a doctor's office is not usually an inviting place."

Hutch shrugged his shoulders and said, "Do you think it looks okay?"

"It does, and I know that lots of patients will come to see you. With Doctor Bernard retired and Doctor Samal leaving for Texas, they won't have much choice. They're very fortunate to have you here," she said with conviction.

"What would I do without you? You believe in this adventure more than I do."

"I know firsthand what you can do, and furthermore, you are the most caring doctor I have ever encountered."

"How would you know?"

"Because I watched you taking care of your aunt, and I thought at the time how fortunate she was to have you by her side."

Hutch met her gaze and smiled. The thought of his aunt brought back the memory of the encouragement she had given him to open a practice in Crystal Grove.

"You're right. I just worry. Once we're open, I'll be fine."

They walked out of the office hand in hand, and Hutch locked the door. They drove in silence to Elodie's place, and once inside the apartment, Elodie made coffee, and Hutch lit a fire in the fireplace. The warmth emanating from the hearth was comforting, and they sat down on the sofa to sip the steaming black liquid.

"We need to figure out where we want to live once we are married," Hutch said, staring into the flames of the fire.

"We can discuss that after the opening of your practice."

"You're right. And I must go. My family is flying in tomorrow and will be staying with me at Aunt Ethel's place. Will you come around after work and meet them?"

"I'll be there after six o'clock."

Once Hutch had left, Elodie walked slowly back to the sofa, wondering what it would be like to meet his parents and siblings. She had been an only child herself, and after her father had left, it had been just her and her mother. For a long time, Elodie had not understood why her father had gone. All she remembered was a long-forgotten feeling of being abandoned. Her mother had never talked about him, and after some time, Elodie had stopped asking questions.

After her mother had passed away, a cousin had told her that her father had allegedly raped her aunt—her mother's younger sister—while she had been living with them. The family had learned of the incident, and wishing to avoid a scandal, they had demanded that her father leave. Her father had complied happily and was never seen again.

Elodie had thought about searching for him but then reckoned it was futile. What was the point of trying to find somebody who did not care whether you were alive or dead? Over time, she had put her parents into one of the little boxes tucked away deep inside her heart.

She was not looking forward to meeting Hutch's family tomorrow evening. She had never told Hutch why her father had left; only that he had left and that her mother had died a few years ago. *I'll just stick to that story*, she thought to herself. She got up and cleared the coffee table, then went to bed.

All the next day, Elodie was busy creating her famous flower arrangements, and she lost track of the time. When Heather came to lock up, she was surprised to find Elodie still working.

"Aren't you supposed to go and meet Hutch's family?" she asked.

Elodie looked up and said, "Yes, after work."

"It is already six o'clock, my dear," Heather replied.

"Oh, I didn't realize it was that late!"

"Go, I'll clean up here. Enjoy the evening."

Elodie thanked Heather and ran out the door. She heard a car horn, and turning around, she saw Hutch waving to her and went over to him.

"I had to pick up some packages from the post office and thought I would pick you up."

"Thanks so much, but I have to quickly go home and change. My work clothes are covered with pollen from the flowers."

They drove to her apartment, and she changed into some dark gray pants and a purple sweater. She pulled her hair up into a bun, grabbed her purse, slipped into her black suede boots and ran downstairs, where Hutch was waiting for her.

When they entered the house, the smell of food wafted through the rooms, and Elodie was instantly hungry. She had skipped lunch because there was so much to do at the store. Hutch's mother had roasted a couple of chickens in the oven, made potato wedges and assembled a huge bowl of salad. The dinner table was set, and after Hutch had introduced Elodie to his parents and siblings, they all sat down and enjoyed a good meal. After a few minutes, Elodie forgot her earlier apprehension and fell into relaxed conversation with Hutch's family, whose warm, friendly manner made her feel that she belonged in their midst—a new feeling to her, alien but welcome. After coffee, his parents went upstairs, and Elodie, Hutch and one of his brothers cleaned up.

"Will you take me back, please?" Elodie asked Hutch. "I have to be up early tomorrow; I have a lot to do at the store."

Hutch was silent on the drive home, and Elodie wondered what he was thinking. When they arrived at her place, he said, "They like you—they like you a lot. I'm so glad."

He turned and leisurely kissed her on her waiting lips. She felt a delicious longing pulsating through her, making her flesh itch with desire. She quickly got out of the car and ran up the stairs. He caught her just as she was opening the door.

"Going somewhere?" he asked with a boyish grin.

She pulled him into the apartment. "Not tonight," she said. "You have to go back to your guests. I'll see you tomorrow night." And she gently pushed him outside and closed the door.

After work the following day, Elodie arrived at

Hutch's place just as he was pulling up. They went in together, carrying the trays of food that Hutch had ordered at the little diner in town. They put the trays on the table, and the family gathered and started to eat. Although they spoke of many things during the meal, the conversation kept coming back to the opening of Hutch's practice scheduled for the next day, and Elodie could see how proud his parents were of his achievement. Finally, Elodie and Hutch made coffee and served the small patisserie pieces his parents had picked up at a bakery run by French nuns. The little delicacies were a huge success, and they reminded Elodie of Paris, where she had occasionally indulged and bought some of these little cakes.

"Tell us about yourself, Elodie," Hutch's mother said, looking expectantly at her.

"Well, as you know, Hutch and I met many years ago, in Paris. We met again here at his aunt's house, when she had a party, and the flower shop I work for provided the flowers."

"Oh, I see! You're the girl who created the flower arrangements Ethel enjoyed so much. She used to boast that she was the one who discovered you."

"She was a very kind lady." Elodie sighed.

"And very wealthy," chuckled his mother. "She left this house and all its contents to Hutch because he liked being here."

Elodie glanced at Hutch in surprise, but he shook his head almost imperceptibly, so she merely said, "That was very generous of her."

"I want to quickly go back to the office and make

sure everything is ready for the opening," Hutch said. "Elodie, will you come with me?"

"Of course."

They drove to the office, and Hutch opened the door for Elodie to enter. She was impressed by what she saw. Everything was polished and scrubbed, and the white coats hung neatly on the coat rack. Elodie exclaimed, "This is the first doctor's office I've seen that actually looks inviting!"

Hutch took her in his arms and swung her around. "This is one of my dreams come true, having my own practice." He smiled.

They locked up and drove back to the house. Elodie went in to say a quick good-bye to the family, brushed a sweet kiss on Hutch's cheek and left.

Morning dawned with a light blanket of glistening snow covering the village. The white winter sun sent forth its cold rays and illuminated the dark trees lining the street. Elodie and Heather walked to Hutch's practice to partake in the festivities. The door was wide open, and they entered to mingle among the many visitors. Heather knew most of them and talked with as many as she could. She was full of praise for the new doctor and told everyone who would listen that her favorite flower girl was going to marry the young doctor.

The opening was a huge success, with many of the villagers signing up for an examination. Hutch was beaming with pleasure. After everyone had gone home, Elodie and Hutch left the office together and drove to the Bonefish Grill, a restaurant in the next town, where his family was already seated at a long table. They welcomed him and Elodie and toasted the great opening.

"There is something else I want to tell you," Hutch began. "Elodie and I are going to be married on Christmas."

"Congratulations!" said his mother, and came around to hug them. "I am so happy for you both. What a surprise—although I must say, I suspected that Elodie was the one." Then, taking Elodie by the hand, she said, "Come, sit by me so we can talk."

Elodie followed and sat down next to her. All through the evening, they talked about the wedding, how she and Hutch had met—first in Paris and then again here—and how they envisioned their life together. Finally, the last plates and cups were taken away, and Hutch got up, saying, "Thank you all for joining us tonight and celebrating with us the start of our new lives together. You are, of course, all invited to the wedding. We'll let you know the details later. For now, I wish you all a good night and a safe journey back home." They waved and left the restaurant to drive back to Elodie's home.

"Want to come up for a cup of coffee?"

"Not tonight, I'm tired. But I'll be around tomorrow morning. We need to finalize our wedding plans." Before Elodie could reply, he had turned and walked to his car. She watched him drive away, then went upstairs, lost in thought. That night, her dreams were filled with beauty and serenity and left her full of hope for the future.

23

Festive Days

THAT FALL, ELODIE and Hutch were busy with their
work, and they spent every free minute they had poring
over the wedding plans. Eventually, they settled on New
Year's Day for the ceremony at Aunt Ethel's house. The
officiant had agreed to the date, a caterer had been selected to prepare and serve the meal and decorate the
house, and invitations were sent out.

On Christmas Eve, Heather closed the store at noon
to give her employees time to prepare for the festive
days ahead. Elodie had bought a couple of Cornish
hens to bake in the oven, together with baked potatoes
and a variety of root vegetables. The night before, she
had made an appetizer of aspic and had baked homemade cookies for dessert. She had moved the table
against the window overlooking the sparkling, snowy
landscape—it reminded her of a Kincaid painting—and

created an intimate setting with Christmas greens and scented candles in different sizes.

When Hutch came home just before dusk, he was surprised and gratified to see how much trouble Elodie had gone through. He looked tired but was very pleased with the way his practice had taken off. He had more patients than he could easily handle himself and was planning to hire an assistant doctor in January.

While Hutch changed into casual clothes, Elodie served dinner. The wine was delicious, the Cornish hens crisp and the vegetables tender. They clinked their glasses and toasted to a wonderful life together.

"I haven't had such a tasty Christmas meal in many years," Hutch exclaimed. "Let's sit by the fireplace and have some coffee and cookies."

"Why don't you make a fire, and I'll make coffee?" Elodie replied, smiling.

While she clattered with the dishes in the kitchen, Hutch lit the fire. The heat emanating from the fireplace filled the room with an exquisite warmth. Soon, Elodie brought a tray with steaming coffee and a variety of cookies and put it on the coffee table.

Hutch took her arm and gently pulled her to him. "You are the best thing that has ever happened to me," he whispered in her ear.

Extricating herself from his embrace, she poured coffee into the yellow stone mugs. She pulled her legs under her and snuggled close to him. They both stared into the fire, watching the hot flames stretching toward the chimney and freedom.

"A week from tomorrow, we are going to be married,"

Hutch said matter of factly.

Elodie looked at him questioningly. "Second thoughts?"

"Of course not, silly. I would not change you for the world." And this time, he kissed her softly on her lips. They drank their coffee, nibbled on some cookies and soon decided to call it a night.

Christmas Day dawned, looking like a bride in a lacy white dress. Big, fat snowflakes were slowly gliding to the ground, joining the million flakes that had arrived before them. The world was silent, the way Elodie liked it. She stood by the window looking down on the street, which could not be seen under all the snow, and the cars wearing white snow caps. Here and there, some animal tracks were visible—deer, probably, looking for food. Suddenly, she sensed she was being watched and turned around to find Hutch looking at her.

"What are you doing up this early on Christmas Day?" he asked.

"Will you come with me for a walk? Please?"

"Okay," he said, and crawled out of bed. They quietly bundled up in warm clothing, complete with woolen hats, scarves and gloves.

When they stepped outside, the bitter cold hit them like a knife. "I think I'll turn back," Hutch moaned.

"Come on," Elodie teased, taking his arm and pulling him after her. A few minutes later, the sun illuminated the snow-covered ground, which shone like a carpet stitched with glistening diamonds. The naked trees with their white crowns lining the street looked like important dignitaries waiting for the old monarch to arrive.

They had not gone far when clouds hid the sun, and the wild snowflake dance started again. "Let's go back," Elodie said. "The weather is not on my side this morning." Hutch was only too glad to oblige.

After breakfast, they drove to Aunt Ethel's house to decorate the Christmas tree. Hutch had had it delivered a couple of days ago, and now it was waiting to be dressed in splendor. They searched the attic and found boxes filled with Christmas decorations. Elodie was amazed at the exquisite glass ornaments, each kept carefully in its little box, that Aunt Ethel had collected over many years. Hutch turned on some Christmas music, and they unwrapped the delicate treasures. They hung them on the waiting tree together with the tinsel, little bells, and candles they had discovered in one of the smaller boxes. Soon, the tree looked quite spectacular, and they stepped back to admire it. Hutch flipped the switch, and the small, drop-shaped lights illuminated the tree and made the ornaments sparkle. A festive but peaceful atmosphere enveloped Elodie and Hutch as they stood there hand in hand, gazing at the Christmas tree.

"Let's decorate some more," Hutch said. "I like the way it makes the room feel."

They continued unwrapping Aunt Ethel's hidden gems. They found beautiful garlands, wrapped in silk paper, and draped them around the entryway, the banisters and the mantel. The tiny lights glistened like snowdrops and gave the house the look of a fairy-tale castle. Elodie had brought white candles in many different shapes and sizes, and they placed them around the rooms.

"Next week, I'll make the centerpiece and the matching smaller arrangements so they'll be fresh on New Year's Day."

"Thank you," Hutch replied, squeezing Elodie's hand.

They took one last look around the rooms, then went back to Elodie's place, had some lunch and spent the afternoon curled up in front of the fireplace.

24

Wedding Bells

TWO DAYS BEFORE New Year's Eve, Elodie took the flower arrangements over to Aunt Ethel's house and placed them on the tables. Pleased with the effect, she was just about to leave when Hutch arrived with the caterer, a local woman who had been recommended to them.

"Good that we caught you," Hutch said. "Anna has a selection of dishes she wants us to choose from."

They sat down, and Anna showed them what she thought would be most appropriate for the occasion and for the guests' appetites. After perusing the choices, they selected as an hors d'oeuvre a seafood salad with shrimp, calamari, octopus, and mussels with lemon and extra-virgin olive oil. Spinach dips with toasted pita triangles, wild mushroom tartlets, artichoke mousse puffs, and miniature Reuben sandwiches would be placed on the side tables for the guests to snack on.

For the main course, they took Anna's suggestion of baby rack of lamb coated in an aromatic blend of fresh herbs and spices with mint jelly on the side, served with a medley of baked root vegetables and golden fried potato croquettes. For dessert, they requested a traditional chocolate wedding cake, and vanilla and chocolate pots de crèmes. In addition, there would be cookies and pralines, together with lots of coffee and tea and after-dinner liqueurs.

"What time do you want the main course to be served?" Anna asked.

"The ceremony is at one o'clock, and it will take no more than thirty minutes. Afterwards, we'll have champagne, so I think we could start with the appetizer at three o'clock," Hutch answered.

"I'll be here early on New Year's Day. If you have any questions, please contact me."

"Will do," Hutch replied, and saw Anna to the door.

When he returned, Elodie was deep in thought by one of the large windows overlooking the wintry landscape.

"What are you thinking?" he asked quietly.

"Just how life seems to be much like a river—it goes wherever it's destined to go. On its way, it joins other rivers, and they continue together for a while, and then separate again somewhere along the way."

"What heavy thoughts today," Hutch said, and took her into his arms. "I won't leave you, I promise."

Elodie looked up at him and smiled. "I didn't mean

anything by it; it was just an observation. But thank you for not leaving me, especially two days before the wedding."

Hutch laughed and said, "Let's go and have some dinner at the little diner you like so much. We can come back here afterwards or stay at your place. Whatever you prefer."

"Let's go back to my place," she replied.

On New Year's Eve, Hutch's family and friends arrived at the hotel where Hutch had made reservations for everybody. They met in the evening for a special dinner at one of the well-known restaurants in town. When the clock struck midnight, they lifted their glasses in a toast, wishing one another a good start for the coming year. Hutch and Elodie left soon afterwards and quietly went home to sleep.

New Year's Day dawned with the sun shining on the newly fallen snow, making it look like a queen's coronation coat twinkling with thousands of tiny diamonds. The world looked peaceful and pristine in its new blanket, a good omen for Elodie and Hutch's union. They had a quick breakfast, then headed to Aunt Ethel's house, where Anna had already set the table and started preparing the food. She had brought her daughters with her to help with the preparations.

Hutch and Elodie went upstairs, where Elodie had made up the master bedroom for their stay. They had just retrieved their wedding clothes from the closet when the snow started falling again. It got instantly darker in the room, and Hutch turned on the lights. Thankfully, it lasted for only a few minutes, and then the sun peeked through the clouds again.

Around half past twelve, the guests started to arrive and mingle, aperitifs in hand; then promptly at one o'clock, the officiant arrived. Hutch and Elodie appeared, he looking very elegant in his dark gray tuxedo, she wearing a simple, cream-colored two-piece suit with matching blouse. She wore her dark hair down, and a fine gold necklace graced her delicate neck. The wedding ceremony began, and in less than thirty minutes, Hutch and Elodie were husband and wife. Elodie gazed jubilantly at the eighteen-carat yellow-gold wedding ring with five small diamonds—a symbol of Hutch's commitment to her—that now shone on her finger. He wore a matching ring without the diamonds.

At the reception, they moved easily among their friends and family, accepting their congratulations. The guests were nibbling on finger foods and drinking champagne from tall flutes. Soon, they were seated at the beautifully set table, and the appetizer was served. Hutch's dad and one of Hutch's brothers toasted to the newlyweds, wishing them a long and happy life together, and all the guests lifted and clinked their glasses. The sound reminded Elodie of Christmas bells. She looked around the table and felt very much a part of Hutch's family. Quietly, Hutch squeezed her hand and whispered, "Welcome to my life and my family." Elodie understood the words he had not spoken. Nobody on her side of the family was present. Nobody knew, nobody cared.

The rack of lamb was a huge success, and everybody ate heartily and drank the pinot noir that accompanied the meal. When everybody had placed their napkins on the table, Anna and her daughters cleared the dishes, brought in the desserts with coffee and tea, and placed liquor bottles in the middle of the table for the guests to serve themselves. When night started to fall, Hutch switched on the electric lights on the Christmas tree and the garlands. Elodie lit the candles in the flower arrangements and on the mantel and side tables. The whole house was bathed in a warm, comforting glow, and a hush fell over the party.

Suddenly, a deep baritone voice filled the room and string instruments struck up a tune that had special meaning to Elodie and Hutch. With tears in her eyes, she turned toward Hutch and whispered, "You remembered." He nodded and took her in his arms. Slowly, he guided her toward the far end of the room, where the furniture had been pushed aside to make room for a small dance floor. They slowly moved to the music, and soon other couples joined them.

Elodie felt light and very much loved. Her eyes shone and her breath came in short gasps. "This has been the best day of my life," she whispered into Hutch's ear. "I will always love you."

When the musicians wished them good night, they realized that it was late and the wedding was over. Two vans from the hotel were waiting to take the guests back to their hotel. Elodie and Hutch said good-bye to their friends and family and went upstairs. Tired but happy, they fell into bed to sleep a well-deserved sleep.

Next morning, Hutch was already up and about when Elodie opened her eyes.

"You're up early," she said. "Any particular reason?"

"I want to take my wife away for a couple of days, provided she can get up." He smiled.

"I like the sound of that—especially the 'my wife' part."

She dragged herself out of bed and into the shower. Soon she was ready and followed Hutch to the car. He started to drive west, and she wondered where he was taking her. After a couple of hours, he stopped in front of a beautifully decorated inn.

"Come," he said, pulling Elodie from the car. A man dressed in a warm winter coat took the suitcase out of the trunk, and Hutch and Elodie stepped inside the inn, where they were greeted by a friendly, roundish woman who showed them to their cottage. Elodie was speechless. A huge fire was burning in the stone fireplace, warming the whole cottage. A soft green sofa with red-and-green striped pillows stood at the far end of the room, green-and-brown satin curtains framed two large windows and on the side tables stood fragile Tiffany lamps. Pots with blooming red amaryllis perched on little wooden stools, and a huge forest-scene tapestry covered one of the walls. The room was bathed in a soft glow, and the faint smell of flowers permeated the air.

Elodie peeked into the other rooms and saw a bathroom with a cream-colored sunken tub, two sinks and a variety of soft towels and lotions. In the bedroom, a canopy bed, covered with a red-and-gold bedspread and toss pillows in matching colors, awaited the tired travelers. Two small windows framed the bed, and a cheery armoire stood against the wall.

Elodie turned toward Hutch, whispering, "This is absolutely gorgeous! How did you ever find this gem?"

"One of my patients recommended it, and I thought you would like it."

"Oh, I do, I do," Elodie replied. She planted a kiss on Hutch's cheek. "How long will we be staying here?"

"Until Sunday. I have to be back at the office on Monday morning."

"That's three nights. Oh, how wonderful! Thank you so much for this wedding present."

There was a soft knock on the door, and a woman's voice said, "Your dinner will be served in about thirty minutes if that's convenient for you."

They had just about enough time to unpack and get out of their traveling clothes before dinner was brought in and placed near the fireplace, on a table already set for two. Delicious smells emanated from several covered dishes, making Elodie hungry, and they sat down and took the lids off the bowls. There were shards of cured meats and cheeses with Parmesan crisps, crab cakes on a bed of arugula with garlic aioli, roast beef with Yorkshire pudding and braised vegetables, and fig pie with whipped cream for dessert. They served themselves and enjoyed the tasty dinner tremendously.

After the meal, Hutch made coffee, and they savored the fig pie while sitting in front of the fireplace. "And how is Mrs. Garter feeling this evening?" Hutch asked teasingly.

"Mrs. Garter is feeling very happy and very amorous," Elodie replied with a smile in her voice.

They clambered into bed, and Hutch took her into

his arms, whispering into her ear, "I do love you, Elodie Garter, and we will have a great life together."

"I love you, too, and I know we'll have a great life."

He wanted to say something else, but Elodie kissed him on the mouth, and they came together for the first time as husband and wife.

When morning dawned, they lazily woke up, showered, dressed and strolled over to the main house, where they ate a sumptuous breakfast with poached eggs on a bed of steamed spinach and a delectable hollandaise sauce, steaming cups of black coffee and slices of sweet rhubarb pie. Later, they walked the narrow streets of the picturesque town and visited the many endearing little shops catering to noisy tourists. They had dinner in a small restaurant off the beaten path and afterwards walked hand in hand back to the inn.

Their idyllic escape passed only too quickly, and soon they were heading back to Crystal Grove and everyday life. Hutch returned to his practice, and Elodie went back to the flower shop.

25

A New Life

ELODIE'S LEASE ON the apartment was set to expire at the end of March, and she was not going to renew it. Hutch thought that they could live in Aunt Ethel's house until they found a place of their own. They were in no rush to find a home, so Elodie slowly moved her things over to Aunt Ethel's house. The few pieces of furniture she wanted to bring would easily fit into a U-Haul truck, and the rest she would give to the women at the flower store. At last, the apartment was empty. She looked around it with mixed emotions—her heart felt both heavy and light. She had many fond memories of this place and felt like she was parting from a good friend. But ahead of her, another life was waiting, and she had no regrets about leaving the old one behind. For the last time, she closed the door, locked it and turned the key in to the landlord.

Hutch and Elodie settled easily into their new life together. Hutch was very busy with his practice and had hired another medical doctor to help him. He was also increasingly sought after for a variety of surgeries at the hospital. Elodie continued working at the flower shop and took over more and more responsibilities from Heather.

One day, Heather called Elodie to her office and made her an astonishing proposal. Heather wanted to retire, and as she had no children of her own, she asked Elodie if she would be interested in purchasing the flower shop. Elodie was taken aback; she had not expected this! The idea was tempting, but she needed more time to think it over. She told Heather that she would discuss it with Hutch and let her know in a few days.

When Hutch came home that evening, Elodie, flushed with excitement, grabbed his hand, planted a kiss on his lips and exclaimed, "Heather wants to sell her flower shop to me. I told her that I need some time to discuss it with you first before making a decision."

Hutch saw her happiness at the prospect of owning the flower shop and replied, "That is great! I'm sure we will be able to work this out, though it will mean long hours at the shop for you."

"I have thought about that, but I love to be among flowers almost as much as being with you," she replied sheepishly.

Hutch laughed, pleased to see his wife so happy.

"I'll tell Heather tomorrow."

The next morning, Elodie told Heather that she

would buy the shop, and they settled on a purchase price and had the papers drawn up. Heather would stay in the apartment above the store until she was ready to move, and Elodie would keep the office as it was. When they announced the change to the employees, there was general applause. They all thought highly of Elodie and were happy that the store would not fall under new management but would continue on as before.

Late that summer, just as the heat was about to break, Elodie suspected that she was pregnant. She took a pregnancy test, but the result was negative. That evening, she told Hutch. Although he had never given much thought to having a family, he was not opposed to the idea and suggested that he examine her at the practice. They went to his office early the next morning so he could run a few tests. When he reviewed the test results, however, he realized that they would never have a family of their own. Elodie had a congenital disorder of the uterus that made it impossible for her to conceive.

When he got home that evening, Hutch told Elodie of his findings, and Elodie looked at him, unable to speak. She had never thought that it would be impossible for her to get pregnant. The news was unexpected, but somehow, she was relieved. Hutch took her in his arms and gently played with her hair.

"You know, it might be better if we don't have children," he said. "We both have our work, and in all honesty, I don't want to share you with kids. I remember my mom was always running after the four of us, taking us places, picking us up and making sure that we were all right. I just don't know how my dad coped with all that. They had very little time to themselves."

"And I," Elodie replied, "was not a happy child. My parents fought all the time, and I was always in their way. After my father left, my mother tried to make up for the lack of love, but it never quite worked. I think you're right—it's better for us not to have children."

During the night, Elodie woke up, and her thoughts returned to the events of the day. *How strange*, she thought, *that I should be unable to bear children. But Hutch and I will manage quite nicely without any.*

Next day at breakfast, she told Hutch that she would prefer to tell anyone who asked when they were going to start a family that they had decided not to have any children. Hutch agreed, and soon his family and friends stopped asking about the new generation.

The next few years passed quickly, with both of them preoccupied with work. They spent as much free time together as possible, and occasionally they flew to Seattle to visit Hutch's parents, who were always pleased to see them. Whenever they could get away, they took a short trip to one of the country's great metropolitan cities—Boston or New Orleans or New York.

Along the way, they sold Aunt Ethel's house, together with most of her furniture. This allowed them to make a large down payment on a new home in Crystal Grove. It was a beautiful brick house located in a woody subdivision, close to Hutch's office and even closer to the flower shop. They spent many a weekend searching for furniture that would make this house their home. They updated the kitchen and bathrooms, and installed new hardwood floors and carpets in the upstairs bedrooms. The den had a huge brick fireplace, and on many a winter evening, they sat in front of the fire, drinking glasses of wine and talking about their days at work.

Elodie ran the flower shop efficiently and it prospered. Heather had moved to a condo in Florida, together with one of her friends, and once a year, Elodie visited her and kept her up to date on the shop. Hutch's practice expanded into new facilities, and he hired several more doctors and nurses. He spent more and more time at the hospital, and Elodie never questioned this—until the phone calls started.

When she would ask him who had called, he would tell her it was someone from the hospital. In the beginning, Elodie accepted this, but when the phone calls became more frequent, she began to have doubts. Hutch spent at least a couple of hours a day at the hospital, and she wondered why they could not discuss any patient issues while he was there. Why call him after hours at home?

But she did not dwell on it; she was busy with her shop and often went to town to meet with vendors and negotiate flower prices. Sometimes, when she came home tired from such meetings, Hutch had dinner ready, and she was always grateful for his thoughtfulness. Elodie's happiness was marred only by the phone calls, which seemed to be increasing in frequency.

One day, with deceptive calm, she asked Hutch who was calling so often.

"It's a former patient," he replied easily. "Her name is

Kanesha. I met her when I took over another doctor's rounds. She and her husband lost their boy some time ago in a traffic accident, and she was being treated for severe depression. Now, he wants to try for another child, but she's not sure she wants to get pregnant again. One day, she confided in me, and I told her she could contact me any time she needed to talk."

Elodie scrutinized him with dark, earnest eyes, wondering if there was more to the story than he was telling her. She did not question him further, though, and he seemed relieved that she had let the subject drop. She could only hope that this intruding woman would get over it and disappear from their lives.

26

Kanesha

KANESHA AND FRANKLIN grew up on the same street on the South Side of Chicago. They walked to school together, did homework together and spent most of their free time together. After high school, Franklin enrolled at the University of Illinois at Urbana-Champaign to pursue his dream of becoming an electrical engineer, while Kanesha attended Illinois State University to obtain a degree in graphic design. After graduation, they got married and lived in the city.

A few years later, when Kanesha was pregnant, they moved to one of the smaller villages surrounding Chicago. They bought an old house by the Fox River that Kanesha had fallen in love with. Together, they renovated and updated the old beauty, keeping as many original details as was functionally possible.

When their boy was born, they named him Taine, a

Maori word meaning "god of light." Taine was a lively baby and grew into a very active toddler. He was immensely curious, and Kanesha quit work to stay home and watch over their little sunshine. Often, they strolled along the narrow river walk, overgrown in some places by wild bushes and tall reeds, or played on the manicured lawn behind their house.

They were a happy little family, and nothing troubled their life until one sunny Saturday afternoon in late summer, when Taine was four years old. Kanesha was busy preparing the river-facing garden for winter, cutting dead plants, covering sensitive roots with mulch, and burying a few bulbs deep in the soft earth, hoping they would bloom in spring after the last frost. Franklin was at his workbench in the garage, making a wooden box for Taine's toys. He was almost done—only a few more nails to add before it was ready for Kanesha to paint.

Both were deeply engrossed in their work when suddenly, the quiet was shattered by screeching tires, car doors slamming and an ear-piercing scream. Kanesha ran toward the front of the house, joined by Franklin, who had emerged from the garage. They looked at one another, a cold realization dawning in their eyes: Taine!

Even before they reached the scene of the accident, Kanesha knew that it was Taine. She was not mistaken. There on the hard gray surface lay Taine's broken body, blood pumping out of his small form and seeping into the cracks in the narrow road. His limbs were twisted at impossible angles, his head cruelly distorted. His little face was unrecognizable. Kanesha slumped to the ground beside him, trying to comfort him.

The ambulance and the police arrived at the same time and took over, the paramedics working frantically over Taine, who was still breathing. But while Kanesha and Franklin watched helplessly, his body stilled and his young soul rose to the heavens. A bloodcurdling scream escaped Kanesha's throat, and her arms flailed uncontrollably in the wind. The world around her tilted and spun as she tried in vain to hold on to consciousness. Franklin's arms around her were the last thing she felt before the black abyss swallowed her. She seemed to fall for a long time into this bottomless void, numb to all sensation.

Later, hushed voices slowly penetrated the fog in her mind, and with lightning speed the realization hit her that Taine—her Taine—was dead.

"Franklin," she whispered. "Taine?"

"He is an angel now," he replied in a tearful voice. "God called him to join him in heaven."

Furiously, Kanesha turned toward him, her eyes overflowing with bitter tears. "He was only four years old! How can a benevolent God kill a four-year-old boy? What is God going to do with him? "

Franklin took her hand and started to say something, but Kanesha violently pulled her hand away. "Don't you touch me! Why weren't you watching him?"

"I thought he was with you in the garden."

Kanesha glared at him with hate in her eyes, then stormed out of the room, leaving Franklin sitting there alone.

The days after the funeral were filled with emptiness, hatred and reproaches. Even months after the accident, Kanesha could not endure Franklin's nearness, and one cold morning, she waded out into the gray river, seeking relief from her pain. Luckily, a neighbor alerted the police, who pulled her out of the freezing water. She was taken to the hospital, where she was diagnosed with severe depression. Her doctor ordered her to stay at the hospital for a couple of weeks under the care of the resident psychiatrist.

One day during afternoon rounds, Kanesha received a visit from a Dr. Garter, who was filling in for her regular doctor. Dr. Garter, taking pity on this young woman who had lost her child, tried to help her and her husband overcome this trial and find solace in one another. He gave her his phone number and told her to call him if she was ever in need of a friend. She was grateful for his help but did not call him for many months, until one night when she was feeling especially desperate. She was going to jump from an overpass. Dr. Garter rushed out and arrived just in time to pull her back from the railing. He drove her home to her husband, whom he advised to get in touch with her psychiatrist immediately.

A few months later, Kanesha called him to thank him for saving her life. The situation between her and her husband was slowly improving. She found it very easy to chat with Dr. Garter, and gradually, he became a part of her life. Whenever she needed someone to talk to, she dialed his number, and once or twice a year, they met for coffee and exchanged the latest news of their lives. It never occurred to her that his involvement with her was anything but professional.

27

An Incident

SUMMER TURNED INTO fall, and soon winter would come, bringing snow and cold weather. It had been a frosty, windy day, and Elodie was looking forward to spending the evening with Hutch in front of the fire she had lit a few minutes ago. It painted the den in dancing colors, and the warmth emanating from the hearth was comforting. She liked the smell of burning wood that permeated the lower level of the house. Outside the window, the first snowflakes were falling from a dark sky and whirling in the wind on their voyage to the thirsty ground.

Elodie was filled with a sense of well-being. She had spent all afternoon cooking a dish perfect for a wintry day. The beef roast was simmering in her scratched blue Dutch oven, emitting a delicious aroma, the mashed potatoes were boiling together with small carrots, and the green beans were waiting for the onion and garlic sauce that would give them their unmistakable flavor.

Hutch arrived home some twenty minutes later, looking terrible. His eyes were watery and shiny—not a healthy shine but a sick, feverish shine—and he was sniffling and coughing. It looked as if the flu had finally caught up with him. Elodie helped him get out of his heavy coat and hung it in the hall closet to dry while Hutch went upstairs to change into a comfortable shirt and pants. When Elodie called to him that dinner was ready, he slowly came downstairs.

"It must smell good," he said, "but I only get a vague odor. My nose is clogged and my head hurts."

"Sit down. Maybe some comfort food will help you," she replied, eyeing him with concern.

They ate in silence. Elodie sensed that his mind was preoccupied with something—something other than his usual work. Whenever he was worried about that woman, his face had a peculiar expression. So, when after dinner he went to his office and made a phone call, Elodie knew that he was talking to her. She tried to ignore it, but the nagging in the back of her mind refused to be stilled. It was not the first time that Elodie was left alone by the fire while he had a lively conversation in his office. He tried to keep his voice low, but a sudden laugh made Elodie perk up her ears. She was hurt, and a slow anger started to build inside her.

Hutch walked back into the den and sat down in his corner of the sofa. He looked at Elodie, his eyes filled with guilt, and tried to start a conversation. She fought to conceal her anger—she was glad that in the light of the dancing fire, her features were obscured—but her monosyllabic answers told him enough. He gave up and turned toward the television to watch his favorite show. The evening passed in silence, each occupied with their own thoughts.

Finally, Elodie got up. "I'm tired," she said. "I'm going to sleep." She walked out of the room and up the stairs. She quickly put on her pajamas and was fast asleep by the time Hutch came up to the bedroom.

She was awakened in the middle of the night by a strange noise. It took her a few seconds to realize that it was Hutch, whispering into the phone. She was unable to understand the words but gathered that it was the hospital calling with some emergency that required his presence. Hutch got up, and Elodie heard him run down the stairs and open the garage door. She fell asleep again and did not hear the garage door close.

As she was getting ready for work the next morning, a wave of apprehension swept through her. Slowly, the events of last night pushed through to her consciousness, and with sudden clarity, she realized that something in her relationship with Hutch had shifted. But she put the troubling thoughts aside, made herself some breakfast and drove to the flower shop. She loved the fragrance of the sleeping flowers and enjoyed taking them out of the deep buckets full of water to create her astonishing arrangements. By noon, she was herself again, and the negative feelings of the previous night had dissipated.

With the holidays approaching rapidly, Elodie had

no time to waste thinking of Hutch's phone calls. She was busy at the shop, filling orders for the special seasonal arrangements her customers had requested. While she was preoccupied with her work, the old year stealthily gave way to the new, leaving the world quiet once again, covered with a white blanket of cold snow. Then, one morning, when she opened the windows, she heard birds chirping and knew that winter's spell had broken and spring was coming.

It was a warm day in early spring, and Elodie was meeting with one of her clients at the village café in the neighboring town. Tables and chairs had been put outside in anticipation of warmer weather, but Elodie preferred to be seated inside. The wind was unpredictable and could still be rather cold. While her client was looking over the proposal for the arrangements for her daughter's wedding, Elodie surveyed her surroundings and, to her amazement, saw Hutch and a dark-skinned woman approach the restaurant and choose a table outside.

Partially hidden from their view, Elodie studied the woman's features. Hutch took her hand and patted it in a familiar manner. Elodie could not hear his words, but the woman must have found them comforting because her face lit up and she smiled. A wave of misgiving swept over Elodie, and she needed all her willpower to listen to her client. The woman had a few questions that Elodie answered automatically. At last, the woman signed the contract and left.

Elodie stayed seated, watching her husband talking to his companion. When they got up, she was stunned to see Hutch take the woman's arm. They left the café and disappeared from Elodie's sight. She was numb with increasing rage and shock, and her breath burned in her throat. She got up, paid at the cashier's and walked to her car in a daze.

What just happened? she asked herself. *What was Hutch doing with that woman? I've never seen her before.* She knew it wasn't one of the nurses or doctors from his office. Suddenly, the realization hit her: *This is the woman from the phone calls.*

She felt a misery of spirit she had never known before. Her world had been turned upside down. *Pull yourself together*, she admonished herself as she drove unsteadily back to the store.

She put the fury that raged within her on ice and entered the store with a smile, saying to the waiting saleswomen, "Mrs. Barbary finally signed the contract for her daughter's wedding." The staff applauded.

Elodie excused herself and walked to her office, where she promptly slumped into her chair. Erratic thoughts chased one another without making sense. *What does this woman mean to Hutch? Is he just helping a friend, or is there more to it than that? Is she even a friend? Why does Hutch never talk to me about her? If he had nothing to hide, why wouldn't he talk to me about her? Is she the woman from the phone calls? How long has this been going on? Do they often meet like this? How can he do this to me?*

A soft knock at the door interrupted this feverish reasoning.

"Come in," Elodie said, putting some papers into a

drawer.

"You have a visitor," the saleswoman said, and Elodie got up and followed her to the front of the store.

"Heather!" she exclaimed. "How wonderful to see you!"

They hugged and Elodie asked, "When did you get in?"

"This morning. I had a few things to take care of in the city and thought I'd come for a quick visit."

They walked through the store, Heather approving of the changes Elodie had made over the years. When they had finished the inspection, they drove to Elodie's home. They went inside, and Heather sat down on the sofa in the den while Elodie made some coffee.

"You will stay for dinner, won't you?" she asked Heather.

"I can't, but thank you for the invitation. Maybe another time. Come sit with me for a while and tell me how your life is going."

Elodie, not wanting to discuss the events of the morning, lightly said, "Life is good. We're both busy with our work."

A shadow flickered across Elodie's face, but Heather did not pry.

"Maybe we should have had children," Elodie said. "Maybe it would have given us some common ground."

"Oh?"

Elodie smiled at Heather. "It's just a fleeting thought." And she told her about Hutch's sister, who had come for a visit some months ago with her two children, a boy of five and a girl of seven. They had loved running around the backyard and playing hide-and-seek in the little wood at the back of the property. One evening, they had been thrilled to see a family of deer majestically walking through the trees on their way to their feeding ground. They had never seen wild animals up close except at the zoo.

Elodie smiled at the images of that visit that floated through her mind. All the same, she was glad that she did not have to deal with children daily. "I guess by now Hutch and I are used to it being just the two of us, and anyway, it's too late to have regrets."

They talked about this and that until Heather checked her watch. "Will you take me back to the store?" she said. "My ride should pick me up there soon."

Elodie drove Heather back to the store, and they waited in the back office until her ride arrived and they said their good-byes. Elodie was still at the store, finishing some paperwork, when the doorbell rang and a customer stepped inside. One of the saleswomen approached her and asked her what she was looking for.

"I'm looking for Elodie," said the elegant woman.

"I'm Elodie," said Elodie, hesitating slightly. The woman looked vaguely familiar, but she was unable to place her. "What can I do for you?"

"I was told that you have magical hands and make unusual flower arrangements; and I do need something quite special," answered the woman smoothly, her face bland.

Elodie pointed to the arrangements displayed in the

vitrine, and the woman picked one Elodie had made earlier in the day.

"I like this one," she said.

Elodie wrapped it up while the saleswoman rang up the sale. Taking the flowers, the woman turned and walked to the door.

"In case you're wondering who I am," she said to Elodie, "I'm Adele." And she left the store without a backward glance.

Elodie stood there as if hit by a lightning bolt, her smile vanished, wiped away by memories of a time long past. She had not thought of Mike in years. He had become a memory she still kept locked away. It no longer hurt, but she did not want to remember it. Adele's sudden appearance made her wonder whether Mike was also in town.

Her thoughts were interrupted by the ringing of her cell phone. It was Hutch, who was on his way home from the hospital and wanted to know if she would join him for a cup of coffee and a slice of pie at their favorite restaurant. She accepted and left the store a few minutes later.

When she arrived at the little diner, Hutch was already seated at a table by the window, and Elodie joined him.

"You look troubled," he said to her.

A melancholy frown flitted across her face, and she shook her head. "Just the usual," she casually replied.

They ordered coffee and Hutch told her about his day. Elodie only heard half of it; her thoughts were miles away, and she had difficulty concentrating on his narrative. Hutch looked at her questioningly, and finally, Elodie told him about Adele.

"Sometimes, the past can be very intrusive," he said pensively, taking Elodie's hand. He did not press the issue. Elodie had told him about Mike and how it all had ended. He did not need to know more. She nervously bit her lip, her beautiful face reflecting her inner turmoil.

"Let's take a drive toward Lake Michigan," he said easily. "That will take your mind off Mike and that ancient history."

"You're right," she answered, sounding unconvinced. But a glance at his honest face gave her pause, and she knew that he wanted to help her overcome this sudden intrusion by Adele.

They spent a couple of hours walking along Lake Michigan, and slowly, the memory of Mike and Adele receded into the background again. Hutch taught her how to throw a flat stone into the lake so it hopped a few times before disappearing into the murky deep. Elodie tried but had no luck; her stones just sank the moment they hit the water.

After a while, she gave up. "I can do many things," she said, "but this is not one of them. Why don't we head back and enjoy a glass of wine on the terrace?"

"That's an excellent idea," Hutch replied.

Stopping at a small grocery store that sold interesting delicacies and wines from all over the world, they bought a bottle of wine from Oregon, freshly baked rolls and some cheese. The smell of the fresh bread permeated the car and hurried them home. They arranged their treasures onto small plates, and Hutch opened the bottle of wine and poured the ruby-red liquid into tall stemmed glasses. He handed one to Elodie.

"A toast to my lovely wife," he said, "and to a long and healthy life together!"

Elodie felt a bottomless peace invading her being as she looked at Hutch. *I must be the luckiest woman on this earth,* she thought, *to be loved by such an incredible, lovable man.* However, the feeling was short lived—pictures of Hutch and the other woman suddenly intruded upon her. She quickly averted her eyes and pretended to have something caught in her lashes. She could not safely face him without betraying her troubled feelings. Hutch did not seem to notice, though, and they settled down to read their favorite papers on their tablets.

Soon, Elodie got up, cleared away the dishes and glasses and put them in the dishwasher. She called to him from the kitchen that she was going upstairs to watch a program on the television in their bedroom.

Cß

A LITTLE WHILE later, Hutch came up and found the television still on and Elodie fast asleep. He turned it off and slid between the sheets. When he tried to get closer to her, she turned away in her sleep, and he wondered if something else had happened today that she had not mentioned to him. But before he could think about it, he fell into a deep and uninterrupted sleep.

28

The Accident

AFTER TWO WEEKS of stormy weather, a crisp Saturday dawned without rain, and Elodie and Hutch decided to clean out the gutters. The leaves from the tall old trees had clogged the downspouts, and the rainwater overflowed and ran in little rivers along the periphery of the house. Hutch got the aluminum ladder from the shed on the side of the property, leaned it against the wall and started to climb. Elodie worried that the ladder was at an unsafe angle, but as Hutch ignored her words, she turned and figured that he knew what he was doing. After working for a couple of hours, they finally arrived at the last downspout.

Again, Hutch positioned the ladder, and this time Elodie shouted so he had to hear. "The ladder is at too steep an angle."

"It's fine," he replied, and climbed to the top. Elodie

watched him while he pulled out the leaves. When his phone started to ring, he reached into his pocket for it. The sudden move made him lose his balance, and clinging to the heavy ladder, he crashed to the ground. His head hit one of the stepping stones with a dull thud, and a small rivulet of blood escaped from the side of his mouth.

Elodie ran and kneeled beside him. His face had an unnaturally pale tint, and his eyes were closed. She stared at him, knowing that she should call the ambulance but unable to move. Feelings of rejection and hurt—hate, almost—rolled over her like waves on a rocky shore. Suddenly, all the pain she had endured in the past seemed to collect in this one moment and paralyze her.

Hutch's hand found hers and pressed it lightly. He opened his eyes and whispered, "I have always loved you, Elodie, and I have always been true to you. You were the sunshine in my life, and I thank you from the bottom of my heart for all the wonderful days and years you spent with me." His eyes closed and his breathing became shallow. Elodie continued staring at him and listened to his heartbeat growing fainter and fainter.

She had no idea how much time had elapsed since the fall, but when suddenly Hutch shuddered and went still, his head lolling to the side, the realization hit her that he was dead. She let go of his hand and ran into the house to call the ambulance. Within minutes, the paramedics arrived and found Elodie kneeling by Hutch's side, holding his hand. They gently took her inside and loaded Hutch's body into the ambulance.

The police had also appeared on the scene, and an officer who knew Elodie from the flower store asked if she could call someone to come and stay with her. Elodie gave her the name of a friend in town and then lapsed into silence.

There was just one thought turning around and around in Elodie's mind: *Hutch is dead, and I let him die!*

இ

A BATTERED CAR pulled up in front of Elodie's house, and Claire got out. Despite her disheveled appearance—long, frizzy hair that made her resemble a comical cartoon character, old blue jeans, a loose woolen sweater of an undefined color, and dark sneakers that had seen better days—Claire was capable and efficient. She sized up the situation immediately and took charge of Elodie, who looked completely lost.

Claire called one of the doctors at Hutch's practice and briefly told him what had happened. He arrived shortly and gave Elodie a sedative. Claire put her to bed, closed the curtains and stayed with her friend until she was sure that Elodie was asleep. Then she descended to the kitchen, where the policewoman was waiting for her.

"I have to ask you some questions," she said, and Claire nodded. "Do you know the couple well?"

"Well enough to know that Elodie is devastated by Hutch's death. They were very close."

"Children?"

"No."

"Any relatives close by?"

"Hutch's aunt used to live around here some years ago, but she passed away before Hutch and Elodie got married."

"What did Hutch do?"

"He has a medical practice in town, and Elodie owns the flower shop not far from here. You know all this, don't you?"

"Yes, but I need to put this into my report. I appreciate your talking to me. What do you think made Hutch fall from the ladder?"

"My guess is as good as yours. I suppose he either slipped or the ladder was not positioned correctly."

"Yeah, that's the way it looks. Well, I think that'll do for now. If we have any more questions, we'll contact you."

"Please do."

"Will you stay with Elodie tonight?"

"Yes, I don't want her to be alone. Please let me know if there are any formalities that need to be taken care of. I don't think Elodie is up to it."

"I will and thank you."

The policewoman collected her papers and left the house. Claire climbed the stairs and looked in on Elodie, who was fast asleep. Then she went back downstairs and called her husband to let him know she was not coming home that night. She found some spare bedding in the hall closet and made up the guest room for herself. Looking in the refrigerator, she found some cheese and jam and toasted some bread, then took her dinner to the den. The big house was silent, and she turned on the television to chase away the eerie stillness.

She thought about the first time she had met Elodie. It had been a cold winter's night many years ago. Both she and Elodie had been taking a gourmet cooking class at a local restaurant. They were both unattached then; Mike had just left Elodie, and the women at the flower shop had given her a gift certificate to take the class as a Christmas gift. Claire had just moved to Crystal Grove and was trying to make friends. When she had seen the advertisement in the local paper for the gourmet cooking class, she had signed up on a whim.

Maybe I'll meet some great guy who's interested in cooking, she had thought. She had made some male friends, but the one she had immediately felt close to was Elodie. When she had first looked into those dark gray eyes, she had felt like she was drowning in a sad pool of misery. She had started to turn away, but Elodie had greeted her in a pleasant, friendly voice, and Claire had approached and said hello. Just then, the instructor had called them to order and the class had started. After a brief introduction, they were assigned to their workstations, and Elodie and Claire had found themselves at the same place.

"Hi again," Claire said. "I hope you're a better cook than I am."

"I don't think so," Elodie replied. "At least, I've never cooked such an elaborate meal."

"Nor have I."

At that moment, the chef had started to explain how to prepare the meal. "As you can see, this is quite an involved dinner, but you'll be surprised at how easy it is to cook it. All it takes is planning, and that has been done for you. The menu plan is on the stove. Look it over for a few minutes, and then we shall start."

Both Elodie and Claire had looked at the menu in astonishment. The eight-course dinner started with cucumber appetizer cups, then avocados filled with hazelnut oil, followed by an arugula-pear-Asiago salad and a vichyssoise. A refreshing lemon sorbet was also on the menu—to cleanse the palate, the instructor told them. The main course consisted of roasted Cornish game hens accompanied by small red potatoes, and green beans wrapped in carrot rings. Dessert was noted as coffee granita—frozen coffee crystals layered in stemmed glasses with whipped cream—which neither of the two women had ever heard of. And to finish the evening, Kahlúa and Irish cream would be served in shot glasses with chocolate sorbet.

"My goodness!" Claire exclaimed. "We'll be here all night."

"It certainly looks that way," Elodie replied.

Claire remembered that the chef had also given them a plan on the sequence of preparation. Following the instructions had made it easy to finish everything at the appropriate time. As they worked, the cook had passed by to taste their cooking and give them tips on how to make it tastier.

I wonder if Elodie ever thinks of that evening, she thought to herself. She tried to pay attention to the movie she was watching, but her thoughts went back in time to a Sunday afternoon when she and Elodie had gone to the movies soon after the cooking class. They had found that they enjoyed each other's company, and from then on, they had gone together to estate sales, concerts in the park, and the great shopping malls in and around Chicago. But when Claire had met Gordon, she had not had much time for Elodie anymore; just coffee or a movie here and there.

When Elodie had met Hutch, the four of them had spent some weekends together, going to the horse races at Arlington, watching a football game, or bicycling. Sometimes they spent an evening together talking, savoring new dishes that Claire and Elodie had prepared, and enjoying shots of whiskey. It was a carefree time when they were young and life was full of surprises and adventure. But after Claire and Gordon's children were born, the two couples did not see as much of one another as they used to. Elodie and Claire still managed to occasionally grab a cup of coffee, and on some weekends, they got both families together and had a barbecue.

Claire sighed, got up from the sofa and put the dirty dishes in the dishwasher. After she had checked that all the doors and windows were locked, she climbed the stairs, looked in on Elodie—good, she was still fast asleep—and went to the guest room. Quickly undressing and slipping into the cold bed, she called Gordon and told him that she would be home in the morning. They spoke for a few minutes, and then Claire fell asleep.

Claire was awakened early next morning by footsteps passing by her door. She hurriedly jumped out of bed and quietly opened the door. There was Elodie, bent and walking slowly down the stairs in her blue-satin dressing gown. Claire slipped into the bathrobe she had found in the guest bathroom and followed Elodie to the kitchen.

Very softly, she said, "Elodie?"

Elodie spun around, her eyes wide open, a feverish tinge on her cheeks. She was holding a cup of coffee in her shaking hands.

Claire approached her and gave her a big hug, whispering, "I'm so sorry for your loss."

Elodie felt like a wooden doll in her arms, and Claire waited for the sobs and tears, but Elodie did not cry. She was very still, her eyes fixed on a point beyond the far horizon and her expression one of mute wretched-ness. Gently, Claire guided her to the sofa and sat down beside her. She was deeply perturbed at Elodie's behavior—she was biting her lip, and a thin droplet of blood had formed on her lower lip. Claire wiped it off with her white handkerchief.

"It was not your fault, Elodie," she murmured. "Hutch fell off the ladder. It was a cruel accident that robbed you of him."

"I know," Elodie whispered, taking Claire's hand. "I just can't see how I can go on without him."

They sat in silence until Elodie said, "I have to notify the authorities, family and friends, and make arrangements for the funeral."

"The police already know, and the doctor has notified

the hospital's human resources department. They called earlier today to ask if they should arrange for the funeral. I said yes, so we just need to call his family and friends. Do you have a list of names and phone numbers?"

"Hutch has it in his office. He always said it was better to be prepared. I'll get it." And Elodie got up to find the list. When she opened the drawer of his desk, she spotted a little black notebook. *I have never seen that before,* she thought, and took it out and put it among the books on the bookshelf. *One day, I'll look at it; just not now.*

She brought the list back to Claire, who had her cell phone ready to make the calls, and nodded to her to go ahead. Claire dialed first the number of Hutch's parents, then some of Hutch's friends, to give them the sad news. She kept the calls short, promising to call back when the funeral arrangements were finalized. When she turned to look at Elodie, she was appalled at her friend's appearance. Elodie was as white as a sheet, her lips looked bloodless except for the spot where her teeth had ruptured the thin skin of her lip, and she was staring blankly into a dark void.

"Come," Claire said, "I'll take you upstairs and put you to bed. You need to rest."

Willingly, Elodie followed her upstairs and slipped between the sheets. In an instant, she was asleep. Claire closed the heavy curtains and left the room.

☙

ELODIE WAS FIGHTING a bitter battle in her mind between right and wrong. She needed to find a way to justify having waited for Hutch to die instead of immediately calling for help. She knew instinctively that she should have called the paramedics straightaway, but why had she not done it? She had felt cast aside by Hutch in favor of this woman who had seemed to play such a large role in his life. Whenever the woman had called, Hutch had had time for her, yet when Elodie wanted to discuss an issue with him, he had been busy. When she had once asked him about his relationship with this woman, he had dismissed her concerns with his most disarming smile, which had left Elodie doubting herself and feeling like an idiot.

Wretched grief took her breath away as the bitter knowledge twisted and turned inside her. To keep her sanity, she resolutely told herself that she had done the right thing—the only thing she could have done under the circumstances—letting him die. She repeated the phrase—*I was right*—over and over again in her mind until she started to feel a tiny release from her guilt. Then she got up, showered, pulled on her black pants and black woolen sweater, and tiptoed downstairs. She found Claire on the sofa talking on her cell phone, explaining the funeral arrangements. Elodie joined her on the sofa and waited until she had finished the call.

"The funeral arrangements have already been made?" Elodie asked.

"Yes, that was the hospital, confirming the time of the service. It will be Wednesday at ten o'clock in the morning. That will give his family time to travel to the funeral."

"Thank you," Elodie replied simply, clutching her hands.

Suddenly, Claire's calm shattered and she started to sob. "I'm so sorry, Elodie. I wish I had words to ease your pain."

Quietly, Elodie put her arm around Claire's shoulder, and the two sat like this for a while, until Claire wiped her tears off her face and got up to pour herself a glass of cold water.

"Do you want me to stay with you tonight?" she asked.

"Thank you, but no, I'll be fine."

"If you need anything, you know where to find me. It's only a short drive." Claire hugged Elodie and left.

29

The Funeral

WEDNESDAY MORNING dawned with a red sky, a chill in the air, and birds ready to fly south for the winter. Elodie, accompanied by Claire and Gordon, sat in the front pew of the church, where the reverend gave glowing testimony to Hutch's life. Beautiful flower arrangements, created by Elodie, adorned the coffin. At the end of the service, a clear voice singing "Ave Maria" rose from behind the organ while the doctors from the hospital who were serving as pallbearers carried out the coffin.

She was mesmerized by the activities and felt a pang of remorse when family and friends proceeded to the grave. She had avoided going to the funeral home, where Hutch's body had been resting in an open casket in one of the viewing rooms. Funeral homes had always depressed Elodie, and she had preferred to meet

Hutch's family at her home. Claire and Gordon had taken care of the visitations at the funeral home, meeting friends and acquaintances who wished to say their last good-byes to Hutch.

The committal service took place at the grave site, Hutch's final resting place, where family and friends gathered to witness the lowering of the coffin and the short formal service in which the reverend committed Hutch's body to the earth. Elodie, with Claire and Gordon standing close behind, dropped a white rose onto the coffin, feeling as if she were watching a solemn funeral scene in a movie. She quickly walked away to the car that was waiting to take her back to the house.

They arrived shortly at the house, where the caterers had prepared delicate finger foods for the mourners. Elodie stood in the foyer, accepting the condolences of the visitors. Claire and Gordon stayed close to her and invited the guests to partake of the food and drink.

After a couple of hours, all the visitors left, including Hutch's family, Claire and Gordon. Elodie sat, alone and exhausted, on the sofa in the den, a sword of guilt lying buried in her breast. The events of the past few days intruded on her mind, and she relived every moment since Hutch had fallen off the ladder. She realized that nobody suspected she had had a hand in Hutch's death.

"Maybe I didn't," she whispered to herself. "Maybe it didn't make a difference whether I called for help immediately or not."

She turned the television on but did not actually watch the screen. She just needed to hear voices to help chase the dark thoughts from her mind. She fell into an uneasy sleep haunted by cruel dreams whose gory details awakened her, soaked in perspiration. She sluggishly pulled herself from the sofa and staggered upstairs, took off her makeup and put on her pajamas. Ever so slowly, she climbed into the bed and with glossy eyes looked at the empty space Hutch used to occupy. She quickly averted her gaze and closed her tired eyes. Sleep was long in coming, and it was not until the wee hours of the morning that she finally fell into a dreamless slumber.

When she awoke, the sun had already risen high in the sky, its warm rays touching her cheek. The picture of Hutch lying in his coffin appeared in her mind's eye, and the warmth she had felt but a moment ago turned to a chilling cold. She got up, took a quick shower and donned a dark-colored business suit and black low-heeled dress shoes. She brewed herself a cup of dark-roast coffee, poured it into her travel mug and opened the garage door. Hutch's car was there, and seeing it brought back another image: Hutch lying on the cold earth, his head bleeding from the wound inflicted by the hard stepping stone, his trusting eyes gazing at her. In a panic, she dropped the mug, and the hot coffee spilled onto the floor, burning her leg.

She turned and fled into the house, realizing that she could not go back to the flower store just yet. Her head was filled with images of Hutch, and she felt like a straw puppet in a dark comedy. Putting her purse down and taking off her shoes, she made herself a fresh cup of coffee and sat down at the kitchen table, her head in her hands, and stared into the void.

Ꮸ

CLAIRE STOOD outside Elodie's door, holding a casserole in her hands, and rang the bell. She was anxious about her friend and had called half an hour earlier to see if she could come over. Elodie had agreed, but Claire had not liked the listless tone in her voice.

The door opened, and Claire bustled in and set the casserole on the cold stove. "I brought you dinner," she said, turning slightly toward Elodie. "I thought you might not be up to cooking for yourself."

Then she noticed that Elodie was all dressed up and asked, "Were you about to go out?"

"I wanted to go to work, but I couldn't bring myself to go," Elodie replied in a whisper.

"You need to rest for a few days. The store is in good hands. Maybe you should go away for a while?"

"I can't," Elodie said without offering any explanation.

Claire went to the kitchen and brewed herself a cup of coffee, then joined Elodie at the kitchen table. She looked apprehensively at her friend. Elodie's eyes were feverish, and when she touched her arm, her skin felt cold and sweaty.

"Come, I'll take you upstairs." She took her friend by the arm, and together they climbed the winding stairs. She put Elodie to bed and drew the heavy curtains shut. In the dim light, Elodie resembled a marble statue, with her veins protruding from her neck and a deadly pallor spreading across her face. Claire tiptoed out of the room and softly pulled the door shut. She was worried about her friend and decided to stay until Elodie woke up.

A couple of hours later, Claire heard footsteps and quickly ran up the stairs. She found Elodie sitting on the bed, still as pale as before.

"Feeling better?" she asked, concerned.

"Much better," Elodie answered quietly.

"Good, I'll go and put the casserole in the oven."

"Please, Claire, I'd like to be alone."

Claire, astonished at Elodie's cutting tone of voice, said, "If that is what you want, I shall leave. I'll come back tomorrow morning."

"That's not necessary," Elodie said. "I'll be fine. I'll take your advice and go to the city for the day."

"As you wish, but if you need me, you know I'm only a phone call away." Claire started to descend the stairs when she heard Elodie say, "Thank you, Claire. I'm thankful for your friendship."

೮೩

CLAIRE LEFT, and Elodie was alone. She went downstairs, unwrapped the casserole and put it in the oven. In a short while, the food was hot, and Elodie served herself a small portion and ate her solitary meal.

30

Thanksgiving

THE REST OF THE week passed slowly for Elodie, and by Monday, she was ready to go back to work. Her employees were happy to see her, but she avoided them as much as possible and busied herself creating flower arrangements. When she was among the flowers, her pain subsided for a while, and she hoped someday it would be for good. The evening came too quickly, and she was reluctant to leave the safety of the flower shop. She dreaded going home to the big, empty house that seemed to be filled with dark nightmares—nightmares of her own making. But eventually, she grabbed her warm coat, locked the door and walked toward her car. Out of the corner of her eye, she saw a shadow moving in the parking lot and was sure it was Hutch coming to haunt her. Her heart beat furiously in her chest, and she started to run.

A friendly voice stopped her in her tracks. "Good evening, Mrs. Garter. Is the flower shop closed?"

"Yes," she replied. She recognized the man standing close to her as an acquaintance of Heather's, and her voice became friendlier. "Do you need any flowers?"

"Actually, yes. I'd hoped I wouldn't be too late. I'm invited to dinner at my sister's house and wanted to bring her some flowers."

"Come with me," Elodie said. "I'll open the store for you, and you can choose something for your sister." Elodie opened the door, and the man followed her inside and selected a small, intimate bouquet Elodie had created only a few minutes ago. He paid, thanked Elodie for her kindness and disappeared into the night. Elodie locked the door again, then briskly walked to her car and drove home.

The big house stood alone among the shadows of the tall oak trees reminiscent of ancient sentinels watching over its inhabitants. A slight breeze rustled through the dying leaves of the almost leafless trees. When Elodie got out of the car, she saw huge rain clouds gathering in the sky, and before she reached the door, the first fat raindrops started to fall. Quickly, she entered the house and was assaulted by the cold that suddenly enveloped her. She had forgotten to turn on the heat before she had left for work. She went to the living room and turned up the thermostat, staring with empty eyes at the flowers dying in their vases. Her gaze wandered from the kitchen to the den, and she felt a bitter cold despair spreading in the cave of her lonely soul.

She went to bed without dinner and fell into a

dreamless sleep. She slept for many hours, but when the alarm clock went off, Elodie woke up exhausted. She felt like a wet towel wrung out too many times. She pulled herself out of bed and into the shower, hoping the hot water would revive her. At first, the spray felt good, but then it started to sting like sharp steel needles, and Elodie finished quickly and stepped out of the shower. She started to dry herself with one of the soft towels hanging on the towel bar. Suddenly, she realized that she was using Hutch's towel and dropped it with a cry.

She hurriedly dressed and ran down the stairs, and left the house. A cold wind was blowing, and she knew that winter was just around the corner. Elodie had always liked winter; she and Hutch had enjoyed many evenings sitting in front of a roaring fire, drinking red wine and munching on nuts and chips. She had cherished these evenings when he would sit with her and tell her about his day at the hospital or his practice. But then, the phone calls had started, and often he had gone to his study to take the call, leaving her sitting alone. On these occasions, she had turned on the television to drown out his voice, inwardly seething with anger and humiliation.

When she arrived at the store, she put these dark thoughts out of her mind and entered the shop with a light smile playing around her lips. She walked to the back office to order some flowers and catch up with paperwork that had accumulated over the past few days. The hours passed quickly, and when the sun was setting, Elodie went to the front to talk to the employees.

Some were already gone as it was past closing time, but a couple were still finishing up the flower arrangements they had started and presently put them into the cooled vitrine. They cleaned up the worktable, swept the floor and got ready to leave. Elodie wished them a good night, grabbed her own coat and left.

When she entered the house, the atmosphere had changed and it felt welcoming again, the way it had always been in the past. She had left a small lamp lit, and now a warm glow spread throughout the house. She put her black leather purse down on the small table by the door and went to the kitchen to prepare some dinner for herself.

Sitting at the kitchen table with a plate of pasta in front of her, she thought of the evenings when she and Hutch had sat there contentedly, savoring one of the meals they had cooked together. Hutch had loved to cook, and often on weekends, he would prepare a delicious meal for the two of them. They would play soft music in the background, and enjoy glasses of wine in beautiful stemmed crystal glasses—a wedding present from his parents—and food served in white porcelain plates they had picked up at an estate sale in Wisconsin years ago. She ate a few bites, then put it back into the refrigerator. She was no longer hungry.

She missed Hutch, his touch, his smiles, and she wished she could hear his clear voice again. She was having difficulty remembering the pitch of his voice. She could see his face clearly, but the voice—the voice had vanished. She sat down on the sofa, turned on the television and watched the screen with unseeing eyes. A piercing pain ripped her insides apart, and she jumped up and almost ran to the kitchen to brew herself a fresh cup of black coffee. Guilt assailed her and caused agony so intense that her breath caught in her throat and she began to choke. She reached for her glass of water and drank the cool liquid in big gulps. Her heart was racing, and the kitchen began to move around her, slowly at first, then faster and faster. She was caught in a maelstrom, her head spinning, and she sank to the floor, unconscious.

How long she had been lying there, she did not know. But when she came back to consciousness, darkness had fallen and the house felt cold and forbidding. Listlessly, she got to her feet and held on to the kitchen island to steady herself. She reached for the light switch but nothing happened. Then, remembering that this switch did not work, she hesitantly walked to the other switch and flipped it on. A soft glow spread throughout the kitchen and den, intensifying with every passing second, but the light did nothing to thaw the frigid cold in her spirit.

I must have been lying on the floor quite some time for the coffee to cool down this much, she thought, and a deep sigh escaped her throat. *What is happening to me?*

She took the cup and reheated it in the microwave, then walked back to the den and tried to follow the movie playing on the screen, with no success. She turned the set off, drank her coffee and went upstairs. She painstakingly took off her makeup, brushed her hair and slipped between the cold sheets. Sleep came quickly, and she slept soundly for many hours.

When dawn broke, she awoke feeling refreshed as she had not been since the accident. *You mean murder,* a little voice in her head said, startling Elodie. She had never thought of the accident in that way. She had only delayed the call to the paramedics; she had not pushed the ladder and caused Hutch to fall. She had never thought of harming Hutch.

So why didn't I immediately call the paramedics? Did I hate him so much that I let him die? Was I so hurt by his behavior that I wanted him to pay for it? The thoughts took root at the edges of her mind, and she was unable to shake them off. They stayed with her all day and all night. Try as she might, these thoughts would not leave.

Will I never be free of them? she silently questioned the night, but no answer was forthcoming.

At the store, Elodie was busy creating her sought-after flower arrangements. Thanksgiving was fast approaching, and she and her team worked long hours to ensure the demand was met.

Claire had invited her to spend Thanksgiving with her and her family, and Elodie accepted gladly. She did not want to spend this festive day on her own. Early on Thanksgiving Day, she went over to Claire's with her hands full with flowers and desserts. When she saw Elodie, Claire's face brightened, pleased to see her friend and to have assistance preparing the traditional Thanksgiving dinner with all the trimmings. Elodie placed the flowers around the house, then went to the kitchen to help Claire.

"Let's start with a cup of hot coffee," Claire said, and

Elodie nodded in agreement. While sipping the coffee, they decided who would oversee what, then began to prepare the meal. Claire's and Gordon's parents were coming, as well as her brother and sister with their families. Elodie knew them all as they had spent time together before. The only difference was that Hutch was not there. The sudden realization brought Elodie to a standstill, and she dropped the knife she was using to chop the onions.

CB

CLAIRE LOOKED questioningly at her but kept silent. She could see that Elodie's thoughts were miles away with Hutch. But as before, Elodie's eyes showed no sign of tears, and Claire wondered whether Elodie had ever cried for Hutch. She did not want to ask but found it strange. She did not know anything about Elodie's past. Elodie never talked about what happened between Paris and her arrival in Crystal Grove, and Claire assumed that it must not have been very pleasant.

The sound of the timer, announcing that the pumpkin pie was done, pulled both women back from their thoughts and into the kitchen. They looked at one another, smiled and checked the pie together. It had a beautiful golden-brown crust and smelled heavenly. Elodie had prepared some custard with whipped cream to put on top just before serving. Presently, they put the stuffed turkey in the oven and busied themselves with washing the vegetables.

Early in the afternoon, the guests started arriving,

and Gordon welcomed them, making sure they all had drinks. The house was filled with happy people, and the delicious aroma of the Thanksgiving turkey roasting in the oven wafted through the house. The green-bean casserole was ready to be put in the oven, and the mashed potatoes were almost done.

"Claire, Elodie," Gordon called. "Come and have a glass of champagne with us."

"I guess we'd better go and oblige," Claire said, smiling and taking Elodie by the hand. They both went into the living room, where Gordon handed each a glass of champagne, and they clinked their glasses.

"The food will be ready in about thirty minutes," Claire said, and her announcement was greeted with applause.

"You have an amazing family," Elodie said as they walked back to the kitchen.

"We're very fortunate. One hears all these horror stories of jealousy and envy among the in-laws. We decided early on that we would always invite both our parents for Thanksgiving. That way, we avoid any unpleasantness."

"Good idea. I suppose that makes everybody happy?"

"It does. Over the years, they realized that we do all the cooking and cleaning up, and they only have to show up and enjoy. Who wouldn't like that?"

Elodie, busy at the sink washing kitchen knives and cutting boards, thought back to Thanksgivings when she was a child. Her mother had always had to prepare everything for her father's family. They had not liked her much, and the feeling had been mutual. They had invariably complained about one dish or another that was not done the way they liked it. She remembered her mother's sour face and lips pressed hard together. Elodie had not liked to play with her cousins, either. They were always rude to her and broke her toys, pretending it was a game.

I assume my grandparents are long dead, and I don't care where those cousins are, she said to herself.

"Elodie," Claire said, "please take the turkey out of the oven and put it on the table to let it rest before carving."

Elodie did as she was asked and heaved the heavy bird out of the oven. The tantalizing smell triggered a rumbling in her belly. She hadn't had breakfast and by now was hungry.

"I can hardly wait to taste the bird," she said to Claire.

Soon the green-bean casserole was nicely browned, and Gordon came to carve the turkey. After the guests were all seated at the long, rectangular table, Gordon placed the turkey in the middle, and Claire and Elodie brought in the other dishes. When everybody was served, Gordon's dad raised his glass.

"With this meal," he said, "we remember all the happy moments we experienced this past year. Let us be thankful for the opportunity to spend this day together, and for the coming year, let us think less about profits and politics, winners and losers, and more about giving and helping others. A toast to the cooks and our gracious hosts."

The guests lifted their glasses and sipped the red

wine. Elodie watched everybody as they ate and was gratified to see that all of them were thoroughly enjoying the food and each other's company. Lively conversation abounded, and Elodie was drawn in despite herself.

When the last person put down their fork, Claire and Elodie got up and collected the dishes. Claire put the dirty plates into the dishwasher while Elodie fetched the leftover food from the table, brought it back to the kitchen, and transferred it into the plastic containers Claire had put out for her. In no time, the dishwasher was humming its cleaning tune.

Claire put on the coffeemaker to brew a special blend for the family while Elodie garnished the pumpkin pie with custard and slightly spiced whipped cream. When she carried the pie to the dining room, she received applause; everybody was eager to get a slice of it. Claire followed with the steaming coffee, and everyone fell silent, savoring the pie and drinking the coffee.

Soon, night had fallen and the guests started to leave. Elodie stayed on and helped Claire and Gordon clean up. When all the dishes were put away, the table cleaned and the floor swept, Elodie said good night to her friends and drove back to the solitude of her home.

31

Christmas

BETWEEN THANKSGIVING and Christmas, the flower shop was busy, and Elodie had her hands full. She was grateful that the extra work left her little time to think. She was the first to arrive in the morning and the last to leave at night. Her flower arrangements hinted at some unspeakable sorrow, but the customers loved them. They could not pinpoint why they found Elodie's creations so attractive; they only knew that they wanted them.

Elodie thought of how Heather had once told her that she could guess Elodie's mood just by looking at the arrangements she was making on that day. When Elodie had asked her how she could tell, Heather had only smiled and said, "Flowers are like children. They feel your mood and behave accordingly."

When Elodie locked the store on Christmas Eve, a

light snow was falling, covering the trees and streets with a thin blanket of snow. The world looked wrapped in silken tissue paper, and the streetlights were like candles flickering in the wind.

When she came up to her house, it looked as if it were covered with powdered sugar, and she felt a painful stab deep in her heart. Hutch had always liked it when the house looked like this.

"Oh, Hutch, what have I done?" she whispered to herself as she entered the dark house. She switched on the lights, and the house filled with the glow of the chandeliers. It was warm inside, but Elodie felt a chill run down her spine and hastily closed the door behind her. With a heavy heart, she put down her coat and took off her winter boots, then went to the kitchen to reheat some leftovers from the previous weekend. She found it easier to cook on weekends and then just reheat the portions in the evenings. She usually took her plate into the den and ate while watching the news. But tonight, she ate at the kitchen table, silently staring out at the snowflakes dancing in the night.

A loud knock at the front door made her gasp, and she debated whether or not to answer. But then she heard Claire's voice and quickly opened the door. There was Claire with her husband and children, their arms full with presents and food.

"Merry Christmas, Elodie," Claire said, giving her a big hug. "Here are some presents for you and some homemade cookies."

"Please come in," Elodie said, and stepped aside.

"Thank you, but not tonight. We're on our way to see

my parents."

Elodie took their gifts and put them on the kitchen table, then returned to the door. "Thank you so much for thinking of me," she said. "You're really my best friends. Have a Merry Christmas, and I'll see you sometime after the holidays."

They hugged, and Claire and her family left. Elodie returned to her kitchen to examine the presents Claire had brought. There were a little silver plate of freshly baked chocolate cookies, another plate of ham, salami and cheese, and some homemade bread. They had even included a small bottle of red wine.

"Hutch," Elodie called out, "come see what Claire has brought." At that instant, icy fingers squeezed her heart as the recollection of Hutch's death pierced her mind like lightning. She gasped in horror and clutched the back of the chair. Her knees were weak and her breathing was labored. Slowly, she walked to the sofa and sat down.

Memories of another Christmas invaded her whole being: a Christmas that she and Hutch had spent at a mountain resort in Vermont a few years ago. She remembered the cozy room with the wood-burning fireplace, the huge, comfortable bed and the charming paintings on the walls. They had dined at a restaurant and later had asked to have champagne brought to the room. Hutch had opened the bottle and poured two glasses.

"To us, and to a long, happy life together," he had said, and they had clinked their glasses.

After a little while, Hutch had carried her to the soft

bed, where he slowly had taken off her clothes, his hands roaming intimately over her breasts, teasing her hardening nipples. Elodie felt her body responding to the memory of that night. She got up briskly, trying to chase away these unwanted thoughts, without success. She stepped outside and let the cold night envelop her, but the thoughts kept on coming.

She turned and walked back to the kitchen, opened the bottle of wine and poured a glass. She drank greedily, then refilled her glass and carried it, together with the bottle, to the sofa. She kept on drinking steadily until the bottle was empty. Feeling dizzy and nauseous, she crept upstairs, slipped into bed without bothering to undress, and fell immediately into a drunken slumber.

When she awoke the next morning, the sun was shining. She had a terrible headache, and slowly the memory of last night came seeping back.

"I can't deal with this," she whispered to herself. "Maybe a hot shower will help."

After she had showered and dressed, she descended the stairs and promptly slipped on the last few steps and fell. When she tried to get up, her ankle hurt terribly, and she was unable to put any weight on her foot.

What am I going to do? she asked herself. *It's Christmas Day and the doctor's offices are closed, but I need to see a doctor.*

She called a cab to take her to the closest emergency room. She had to wait a couple of hours until she was seen by an intern, who diagnosed a sprained ankle. He put a splint on her left ankle and sent her home with a bottle of painkillers. After the cab had dropped her off at her house, she made herself a hot cup of coffee and hobbled to the sofa, spilling some of the coffee. *What a way to spend Christmas*, she thought. She turned on the television and watched one episode after another of her favorite show until darkness enveloped her. Then she got up, being careful not to put any weight on her foot, and limped to the kitchen. Opening the refrigerator, she took out some of the savories that Claire had brought the previous day, prepared herself a small plate and took it back to the sofa, where she continued her binge watching. Before she went to bed, she took a painkiller and slept peacefully, without any of the frightening dreams that sometimes plagued her.

A few days after Christmas, Claire dropped by and chided Elodie for not calling to tell her about the accident. "You come stay at my place now so I can take care of you," she said, and without waiting for an answer from Elodie, she went upstairs, packed a small bag and guided Elodie to her car.

Elodie tried to protest but it was useless. "You stay until after New Year's Day, and then we'll see how you're doing," Claire said on the drive to her house.

Elodie enjoyed her stay with Claire, Gordon and their kids and was glad that Claire had insisted on her spending the festive days with them. Her ankle was healing nicely, and by the time Claire took her back home, she was feeling much better.

She called her assistant at the flower shop and told her that she needed another week of rest. When she returned to work, the splint had been taken off, and her ankle was healed. She immersed herself once more in creating flower arrangements, and the weight she had felt since Christmas slowly lifted off her shoulders. Life became routine again and she was glad.

32

Years Passing

ELODIE'S DAYS resembled one another—days turned into weeks, weeks into months, and before she realized it, a few years had passed. She had made new friends and was going out with a handsome man from the city. That day, they were going to meet in the neighboring village for lunch. Elodie arrived early and ordered a Coke while she waited for him to arrive. Suddenly, she felt a tap on her shoulder.

"Mrs. Garter?" a dark-skinned woman said. "You are Mrs. Garter, aren't you?"

Elodie looked at the woman with a shock of recognition. It was her—the one Hutch had been so involved with. Elodie felt an urge rising in her to slap the smiling face and yell that, because of her, she had let Hutch die. But she simply nodded.

"I am so sorry for your loss. Dr. Garter was an

exceptional man, and without his help, I would not have survived the loss of my child. You see, I was at the hospital being treated for severe depression, and one day your husband made the rounds. He spoke to me kindly and promised to return after his shift was over. I did not believe him, but late that afternoon, he came back and listened to my rantings. I was furious at God, at my husband, at myself, and I blamed everyone for the death of my child. Dr. Garter was patient with me and would come by almost every day.

"When I was discharged, your husband gave me his phone number to call whenever I needed to talk to someone. In the beginning, I didn't dare call him, but one day, I was ready to jump from a bridge and called him to tell him. He convinced me to wait for him and arrived in time to pull me back from the abyss. From then on, I called him whenever I needed someone to listen to me."

Elodie was silent, shuddering inwardly as she listened to the words with rising dismay. The woman did not notice Elodie's agitation and continued with her story.

"I also want to thank you from the bottom of my heart for letting Dr. Garter see me at a moment's notice. He really saved my life more than once. After I got better, we moved away and have been living in Atlanta for the past few years. I came to visit family here and was told about his fatal accident."

Elodie stared at her mutely with ice spreading through her veins. Thankfully, at that moment, a dark, handsome man came looking for the woman, and they both left. Elodie closed her eyes, feeling utterly miserable. Slowly, she got up and left the restaurant. She walked to her car in a daze, not hearing her date calling after her, and drove home with unseeing eyes. Mechanically, she opened the garage door, drove her car in and went into the house. Thoughts, jagged and painful, swirled in her mind, and the words the woman had spoken still echoed in her mind.

"Could it be that there was nothing between her and Hutch? That it was all in my head?" she whispered to herself. "Did I let Hutch die for nothing?"

She flung out her hands in simple despair and sat down at the kitchen table, her head between her folded arms. Her world had suddenly lost its luster and turned cold and gray, despite the warm summer afternoon. Immense guilt engulfed her as she went over the events of that fateful afternoon that had cost Hutch his life. The solace she had always found in believing in her righteousness had been taken away by the woman's revelations.

"I had no right to let him die. I should have called for the paramedics immediately. Why, oh why, did I hesitate and wait until he closed his eyes forever?"

Assailed by a terrible sense of bitterness and regret, she paced back and forth on the carpet until she was exhausted and emotionally drained. At one point, she realized that night had fallen and the house was dark. She climbed the stairs and slipped between the sheets. A sensation of intense sickness and desolation swept over her, and she longed for sleep to come and deliver her from her torture. However, she tossed and turned for hours before finally falling into an uneasy sleep.

When morning dawned and released Elodie from her uncontrollable dreams, she was drenched in cold sweat, and her head felt like it was split in two. With great difficulty, she dragged herself out of bed and into the shower. The cool water ran softly down her body, taking some of the tiredness away, but the headache persisted, and she felt a sore weariness centered in her chest.

Slowly, the memory of the words spoken by the dark-skinned woman seeped back into Elodie's mind and poisoned the day for her. She called the flower shop to tell them she was coming down with the flu and would be unable to come in today. She tried to shake free of her disturbing thoughts by cleaning the basement. She moved boxes from one side of the basement to the other, swept the floor and washed the one window covered by cobwebs. After several hours of this arduous work, Elodie ascended the winding stairs and ate a lunch of canned soup and a slice of wheat bread. She sat at the kitchen table and stared out into the backyard without seeing the clouds gathering in the sky, threatening rain.

She was pulled out of her numbness when the doorbell rang. It was Claire.

"I passed by the flower shop and was told you didn't come in today. Are you okay?" she asked, concerned.

"I'm just a bit under the weather," Elodie replied, sounding tired.

"I have something in the car that I thought you might like," Claire said.

"What is it?" Elodie asked politely. She wanted to be alone and hoped that Claire would soon leave.

"I'll get it for you," Claire replied excitedly. She went to her car and came back holding something furry in her arms, which she laid gently into Elodie's lap. It was a fine-boned white Angora kitten with a long, silky coat and plumed tail.

"Oh, Claire," Elodie exclaimed. "She is beautiful and so soft. Is she for me?"

"Yes, an acquaintance's cat had a litter of kittens, and I thought you might like one of the cute fur balls."

"What type of cat is she?" Elodie asked, smiling.

"A Turkish Angora."

"How funny, I always wanted a white Angora cat but never got around to actually getting one. I know that they can be willful and demanding cats. I'll keep her inside where she'll be safe."

Elodie, looking into the kitten's green eyes, said, "Your name is Samara." Then she turned to Claire. "I have to get all the supplies a cat needs. Will you come with me to buy the things?"

"Sure," Claire replied, "let's go."

"What should I do with Samara?"

"I have a cat kennel in the car. I'll get it, and we can leave her here." Claire fetched the kennel, and when they put Samara into it, she promptly went to sleep.

The two women took Claire's car and drove to the nearest pet store, where they found all the items needed for a kitten. With their arms full of cat gear, they returned within the hour to find Samara still asleep. They put the food and water dishes in a corner of the sunroom, spread the colorful cat pillows here and there, and even set one on the sofa next to Elodie's favorite spot. The litter box was installed in the powder room, hidden by the vanity. Elodie stored the toys in the pantry until she needed them.

"I'll leave you with Samara," Claire said. She hugged Elodie and left.

Elodie went back to the living room and peeked at Samara, who was just waking up. She opened the kennel door, and the tiny animal hesitantly crawled to the entrance. Elodie waited until she was out of the kennel, then gently picked her up and set her on one of the pillows nearby. Quickly, Samara pounced on the toy that had been placed there for her and started to play with it. Elodie watched her for a long while, her thoughts with Hutch, who would have liked to have an animal. There it was again: the agony, the bitter regret and the stabbing pain deep inside her.

When Elodie turned in for the night, she put Samara in the kennel, carried it upstairs and set it on the floor beside her bed. She was awakened at first light by miserable sounds coming from her bedside. It took her a moment to realize that it was Samara, asking to be let out. She quickly got up and took Samara downstairs to the litter box to relieve herself while she filled the food and water dishes.

She watched the little animal nibbling at the food and daintily lapping up the water with her small pink tongue. She picked her up and cuddled her in her arms, whispering, "I'm going to take you to the store. You can stay in your kennel until you're used to your surroundings, and then you can have the run of the place."

When Elodie took Samara to the store, everybody commented on the cute, fluffy kitten. As Samara grew, Elodie set up a little playpen for her to keep her out of mischief. Elodie and Samara fell into a routine that suited them both, and the days quickly turned into months. Yet despite the cat's companionship, as the months became years, the heaviness that weighed on Elodie's heart grew ever more burdensome. She no longer fought the pain deep inside her but accepted it as her punishment. She stopped going out with her friends for dinner or to the movies, letting them believe that she did not want to leave the cat. Elodie hid the true reason from them and suffered in solitude.

When Samara was no longer a young cat, Elodie, feeling a deep tiredness in her soul, sold the flower store and retired. Not having any incentive to care for herself any longer, she let her hair go gray, wore the same clothes most of the time and rarely left the house. She had the grocery store deliver food to her door and ordered other necessities from the Internet. Occasionally, she walked in the garden that Hutch had so loved, but the flowers were no longer blooming, and some native species of plants had taken over. She no longer cared.

33

The Last Night

ELODIE DID NOT FEEL Samara jump on her lap. Her mind was far away, and she realized that the deep, gripping pain in her heart had ceased, and she felt young and light again. Looking around her in wonder, she saw myriads of colorful flowers blooming and honeybees busily gathering nectar. Birds were joyfully chirping in tall trees laden with fruit, and her heart was singing with them. She tried to get up from the bench and walk around the beautiful garden, but her feet would not move. Then she spotted Hutch coming toward her, and she stretched her arms toward him, waiting for his embrace.

ଔ

THE NEXT MORNING, a neighbor found her, covered

by a white blanket of snow. He called the paramedics and the police, who arrived simultaneously and walked to the back, where Elodie was still sitting on the bench. They quickly established that she had died of natural causes: the night had brought the first frost, and Elodie had frozen to death. On her lap was an ice-encrusted white cat. She had followed her and been caught unawares by the cold. Elodie's face looked peaceful, almost smiling, and a lonely tear was frozen on her left cheek.

The End

ABOUT THE AUTHOR

Born and raised in Switzerland, E.B. Sanchez now lives with her husband, sons and a spoiled black lab in a little house on a postage-stamp-sized lot in California.

CONNECT WITH E.B. SANCHEZ

Follow on Twitter:
twitter.com/ebsanchezauthor

Friend on Facebook:
facebook.com/ebsanchezauthor

Subscribe to blog:
ebsanchez.com/blog

Website:
ebsanchez.com

BOOKS BY E.B. SANCHEZ

Ernestine
Elodie